DEMON TOUCHED

SKYE MALONE

Demon Touched
Book One of the Demon Guardians Series
by Skye Malone

Previously published as
TOUCH ME: Book One of the Demon Guardians Series

Copyright 2015 - Skye Malone
Published by Wildflower Isle | P.O. Box 129, Savoy, IL 61874
www.wildflowerisle.com

ISBN: 978-1-940617-75-6

Library of Congress Control Number: 2016952416

Cover design by Karri Klawiter
www.artbykarri.com

Proofreading by Monica Bogza
www.trustedaccomplice.com

Find out about all new releases:
Join Skye Malone's mailing list at skyemalone.com/mailinglist!

AUTHOR'S NOTE

This title consists of three novellas that were previously
published together as
TOUCH ME: Book One of the Demon Guardians Series.

If you have already read Touch Me (or novellas Touch Me
1, Touch Me 2, and Touch Me 3), then you have already
read this book.

The Demon Guardians Series
The Awakened Fate Series
The Kindling Trilogy

PART I

1

"I *PROMISE*," RUBY ASSURES ME, VISIBLY TRYING NOT TO laugh, "you're going to love this place."

Tugging at the hem of my entirely too-short dress, I eye the scene ahead of us warily. The dark city street with rain-slicked and glistening concrete. The innocuous steel door on a brick wall ahead, so easily overlooked during the day. The neon shape above it, glowing blue and twisted into some esoteric symbol I can't identify. No name. But then, silly things like a name over the door aren't needed to make a place like Temptation popular.

"I don't know…" I shake my head at the crowds already lined up between the red velvet ropes and brass stanchions. I can feel the music from inside the club pounding past the walls, like the dull thud of another universe trying to break into this one.

Ruby rounds on me, catching both my arms in her hands. Her dark hair is twisted up in some elaborate-yet-effortless design, and her skillfully applied makeup only accentuates her flawless skin and dark green eyes.

Dark green eyes that are currently glaring at me. "Cait, *live* already, okay? Seriously. If you're old enough to drink, you're old enough to have a life. It's *probably* a law."

My lip twitches. I can't stop it. When the heavens made Ruby, they must've been running a surplus on confidence and take-no-shit mentality.

It helps. I nod.

She smiles. "Good." Spinning on her black high heels in a way that would certainly end me up with a broken *something*, she starts down the road again, her hand gripping my arm to make sure I don't reconsider.

Half an hour later finds us through the line and standing at the door. The bouncer regards us, his face inscrutable and his meaty arms crossed over his chest. I swallow hard. He could probably break someone in two with those things. His eyes scan over Ruby, taking in her cocksure smile and supermodel body, and then skip to me. I try not to run from the scrutiny. I'm average height, brown-haired as if God dumped hot chocolate on my head, and several galaxies over from supermodel on a good day. If Ruby hadn't forced me into this tight little green dress, what clothes I own probably would have gotten me laughed out of the line long before we made it this far.

His gaze pauses on me, considering, and then he jerks his head toward the steel door. Ruby practically hauls me past him to get inside before he changes his mind.

The music hits us like a blast wave when she tugs on the handle and the door swings wide. The black walls of a hallway greet us with pinprick lights overhead that do nothing for the darkness. And on the other end...

I try to keep my eyes from widening. I want to pretend like I come to these places all the time, not stare around like a tourist. But it's difficult. Lights shine like stars over the glistening bottles and long mirror of the bar. People crush up against the counter, waiting, flirting, shouting orders. Amid the crowd, I can see tall tables dotting the room, all of them taken, while music throbs through the space like a giant's heartbeat. The air is bizarrely cool, though, as if someone's turned the air conditioning on high. It makes the hairs on my arms stand on end.

"You want something?" Ruby shouts to me with a nod to the bar.

I shake my head. Unlike Ruby, who—legal or not—has been drinking forever, I rarely ever have alcohol. It's sort of my thing. Regardless, I suspect I'll stand a better chance of surviving this sober. "You?"

She considers for a second and then grins. "Let's go dance first," she yells.

I wish I'd gone with the drink.

Taking my hand, she pulls me with her, weaving through tiny spaces in the crowd, and in only a few moments, we've left the crush behind to run headlong into a railing that separates the higher levels of the club from the dance floor below. Multicolored lights and glowing lasers spin across the dancers—hundreds of dancers, all of them a churning throng of arms and heads and moving bodies. Black concrete walls surround them, and lights flash from the DJ's high perch on the opposite side of the space. White smoke drifts around the crowd, emanating from a fog machine I can't find, and my eyes can't focus on anyone in particular—though the throbbing music doesn't help.

Ruby tugs me toward the stairs. I clutch the brass banister while we descend the steps. She glances back, tossing me a bright grin when we reach the horde.

I attempt to return the smile. I've never been a good

dancer. Hell, I've never been *any* kind of dancer, good, bad, or otherwise. Freshman year of high school, my one and only dance featured me standing in a corner, wondering when I could get home to the fantasy novel I had hidden under my mattress lest my stepmother find it. Three years into college, barring the fact I now live in a cheap apartment rather than at home, not much has changed.

But then, this is Ruby's twenty-first birthday. And this is her birthday present. Us, out at a club, theoretically having a good time.

I try moving with the music. I try to imitate Ruby's effortless grace.

I probably look like I'm having a seizure.

A grimace twists my face for a brief moment before I choke it back again. No, I'm going to do this tonight. Dance. Have fun—or the closest approximation of it I can muster. And if Ruby teases me about it later, so be it. This is still for her. My improbable best friend. The one to whom I owe most of the good moments of the past five years.

And you know what? It's actually not that bad.

Incredulity flickers through me. We're deeper in the crowd now. The atmosphere is sweltering, and people are crushing against me from all sides, but it almost doesn't matter. This sort of *is* fun. The energy of the people. The pounding rhythm of the music. The lights overhead, spinning and sparkling on the fog that surrounds us. It's really thick, that fog. People blur in it, twisting in and out of sight like ghosts while the music throbs and my blood pulses to its beat.

I realize I'm smiling. Some tall, blond-haired guy is all over me now, and against all reason, I can't find it in myself to care. It's electric, his hands sliding down my hips. The heat of his body and the hardness of his crotch pressed to my backside. I know I should be freaking out. At any other time, I *would* be freaking out. This isn't me. I've never done anything like this. But the fog is growing thicker and nothing else matters. I grind my body against his, relishing how alive I feel, and then spin away.

Because there are others here. So many others, and I want to dance with them all. I move on to the next guy. Brown-haired, this one. Shorter too. He grabs my ass and pulls me close, and the process starts all over again.

My pulse is racing. Holy crap, this is *exhilarating*. Why'd Ruby never tell me dancing felt like *this*?

I twist with the music, slipping away from the brown-haired one, grinning like a fool.

Dark eyes meet mine.

Everything slows like the world melts into molasses, and in it, I'm stuck. A guy stands in front of me, his body only inches away, and suddenly, he's the only one in the room. The dancers fade into shadows and mist. The music is the low thrum that underscores the world. And there's just him. Dark skin, the darkest I've ever seen. Sculpted arms hinting at a strong body, as if everything of him is muscle and sinew. He's about my age, at least six-foot-three if not taller, and easily the most gorgeous man I've ever laid eyes on. And he smiles like he knows me. Like he's saying hello.

His hand reaches out. Brushes a shadow, a girl, and shimmering mist ghosts away from her to caress his arm like a lover. His smile broadens.

The mist absorbs into his skin.

He nods to me, still friendly. Still like we're acquaintances who've simply run into one another on the street.

And then he's gone into the shadows and the crowd comes rushing back again.

I gasp. Bodies buffet me on all sides, crushing me, and my exhilaration shatters. The music is too loud. The lights spin like deranged kaleidoscopes, blinding me. I'm hot, coated in sweat, and the emerald-green dress is glued to my skin. My pulse is flying, but my body keeps moving like it can't help itself, like it's lost to the rush of swirling lasers, pounding music, and fog.

Fog that's pouring into me.

My eyes go wide. Flecked with sparks of color and light, clouds of it rise from the dancers like mist over a pond. Tendrils stream away from those nearest to me, moving like charmed snakes to coil around my body, slipping over my dress, my skin, and then vanishing inside me.

It's *so* not a fog machine. Sweet God, what's happening?

My pulse ratchets higher. I have to get out of here.

Frantic, I strain to see over the crowd, struggling to find my bearings and the staircase alike. And it's there. A million miles and one dance floor away.

I forge through the crowd, shudders starting to overtake me. I hear shouted protests from the people I shove aside, the cries inarticulate and meaningless amid the music. But the mist is still coming, rushing in from everyone I pass.

And it feels so good—hot and burning like energy being poured directly into my veins. Like life itself, and I can't stop it. My hands are screaming at me to let them just pull people close. Draw this in. Fill myself with this intense rush till everything fades away.

I think I'm going to throw up.

The end of the dance floor arrives. I grasp the banister like a lifeline and haul ass up the steps. The crowd at the top isn't as bad. The mist on them isn't as thick. But it starts toward me all the same when I come near.

My eyes dart around. The way we came in is on the other side of eternity, and there are too many people in between. But to my left, a red exit sign glows dimly above a second way out.

I bolt toward it. The crossbar thuds beneath my hands, and then the cold night air hits my face when the door flies open.

I stumble out into the alleyway. The next building is crushed up close to this one. There's barely six feet of distance between them. My hands catch me on the far wall, scraping on the brick, and rough breaths rasp into my lungs. A strange symbol glows on the wall, and for a moment, I think it's made of neon tubes, but I'm not that lucky. Formed only of blue-green light, the bizarre marking shimmers like it's part of the brick, and God only knows what it means. Meanwhile, energy pulses through me, beating in time to the music at my back. Heat is there as well, despite the cool autumn air. My body throbs with its strength, flashing hot and cold while the hairs on my skin rise.

"Cait?"

I look over my shoulder at the sound of Ruby's voice. She's standing with one hand on the doorframe, staring at me in horror.

Fog twists around her, white and ghostly with a thousand colors flickering inside. It's fainter than it was on the other people in the club. It seems to be fading into nonexistence. But when she starts down the step from the door, tendrils of it still move ahead of her, twisting toward me like children begging to be taken in from the cold.

With a strangled cry, I retreat fast, my hands rising as if to defend myself. "Stay back."

She stops, a worried and confused look on her face. "Cait, what's wrong? Did somebody try to hurt you?"

I shake my head. I can't answer. How the hell do I explain? It doesn't matter either, because those tendrils are coming closer, brushing my skin now, and oh damn, they feel good. Hot and incredible and making my entire body flush.

Ruby falters, an alarmed look crossing her face like she's picking up on this. Like, even though she hasn't given the *slightest* sign of seeing the mist, she still feels something happening too.

A ragged breath leaves me. Oh God, I have to get out of here *now*. "Stay away. Please, Ruby. Please just stay away."

She doesn't move. The tendrils lose contact with my skin.

I run.

"Cait!"

I hear her shout, but I don't stop. My strappy sandals slap the wet concrete, and the wind is cold on my face. The alley falls behind me, and the next street too, but I keep going. My brown hair is soaked with sweat and turning icy where it bounces against my bare shoulders. I don't know where I'm running.

I'm not sure I care.

I skid around a corner. Another street lies ahead. Another alley beyond it, cast in shadow from the bright street lights on the road. I tear toward it, wanting to hide so that maybe I'll wake up from this nightmare.

The black guy from the club steps out of the alley

ahead. The friendliness in his gaze is gone. Wary alarm is all that remains.

But he's *here*. I've been running like hell; he *couldn't* have gotten all the way around me in the few minutes it's been.

I slam to a stop. His eyes go wide.

And that's when the car hits me.

2

My alarm clock is broken. The beeping sounds all wrong.

"—lucky to be alive," a man is saying in the distance. "The damage—"

"Oh please, she's fine. Look at her. Barely a scratch."

"Her injuries are more than a *scratch*, Mrs. Faire." The man's voice is labored. "Your daughter—"

"*Step*daughter."

"Your *stepdaughter* was hit by a *car*. You need to be prepared for the fact it may take time for her to—"

"What? No. You doctors just want to use up every penny my husband and I have left in medical insurance. What are those bags, huh? IVs? This is nonsense. You're just keeping her unconscious so you can—"

Something jostles on my arm. It hurts like needles in my skin. I wince, trying to make it stop, but my muscles don't want to work.

"Mrs. Faire, you can't—"

"Cait?"

Ruby. Relief hits me, followed instantly by terror. Ruby shouldn't be here. She needs to stay away. There was some important reason she needed to stay away.

It slips through my grasp.

Light pierces the blackness as my eyelids creep upward. A blur in front of me resolves into Ruby's face.

She smiles. "Hey."

I try to speak. My voice is a croak.

My stepmother appears. Her straight red hair is lashed back into a severe ponytail, and her blue eyes are glinting pinpricks of anger—at me or the doctors, I can't be sure. Probably both. "And just what the hell were you doing out on the road at this time of night, Caitlin Jane?"

Desperately, I turn my gaze to Ruby. I don't know what she's said. A long black coat covers her, though, the thing buttoned up to her neck to hide any trace of her dress. My own dress is gone, replaced with a pale green hospital gown.

It's a good sign. Hopefully, anyway. Because if Arlene finds out I've been at a club…

Slut. Skank. Just like your whore of a mother.

The doctor saves me from answering. "I'm going to have to ask you both to leave now," he says, a tinge to his voice like—in my stepmother's case, at least—the idea pleases him to no end. "Caitlin needs—"

"Don't you tell me what that girl needs," Arlene begins.

"Mrs. Faire, you have to go. The nurse will show you to the waiting area where—"

"Oh, so you can charge us for that too? I'm not—"

She does leave, though. Complaining is her style, not getting thrown out on her ear. Her voice fades down the hall, and she's still arguing with a nurse all the while. I close my eyes.

"Cait?" Ruby asks.

I open them again at the sensation of her taking my hand.

A bolt of panic shoots through me. Touching. Something bad about touching.

Ruby doesn't seem to notice. "I'm so sorry," she says, casting a nervous glance to the hall and keeping her voice down. "If I hadn't asked you to go out tonight—"

I shake my head. The motion makes my brain rattle.

She looks unconvinced, but she nods all the same. "I'll see you soon, okay?"

I manage a smile, and when she releases my hand, I let out the breath I've been holding.

The doctor comes back over, one of those pleasant, bedside-manner-type smiles on his face.

I swallow hard. "What happened?" My voice is a whisper. It's a miracle he can hear it at all. Or maybe he just does this a thousand times a day. But either way, he continues to smile.

And begins to tell me.

◦⁀◦

I'M STILL AWAKE HOURS LATER. THE NURSES ARE GONE. THE doctor too. Moonlight pours through the window at my side—the window on the seventh floor of the hospital where I've been taken after the emergency room was done with me. Kept overnight, they said. Observation.

Because I was hit by a car.

The driver was okay, though the sedan itself was a loss. The man had slammed into a light pole after swerving to avoid me. But the glancing impact had still banged me up terribly. I was lucky, though, the doctor said. I got away with some scrapes, a couple of dark bruises, and a nasty bump to my head. It could've been broken bones.

I shift around beneath the stiff white sheets. A blue cotton blanket covers them, too warm for me even in the cool hospital air. I'm not sore, not really. The painkillers are working their miracles, even if they might be to blame for the blur of my memories. I can't remember much of what happened before the car struck me. Just fragments that make no sense, tied to emotions that seem out of place. Unease. A blond guy. Exhilaration. Sparkling lights. Terror. Ruby's face.

It's making it hard to sleep.

A mewling sound breaks the silence, like a kitten seeking its mother. I glance toward the bed on the other side of the curtain dividing the room. A girl is there; I saw her briefly when the nurses pushed the fabric aside to bring me some pills. She's maybe eighteen, with glittering makeup like she's just come from a party. No one would tell me what is wrong with her, though. Something in their refusals makes me wonder if they know.

The mewling gets louder. More desperate.

"Hey," I whisper. "You okay?"

No change. I consider calling a nurse.

I push aside the blankets instead. She could just be having a nightmare.

My feet touch down on the icy tile floor, and my legs wobble briefly when I stand. A livid bruise discolors my right thigh where the car struck me, and motion sets it to aching, but after a moment the pain fades. I set off around the bed, one hand to the mattress to keep me stable.

I grab the edge of the curtain. "Hey, are you—"

The dark-haired girl is writhing on the bed, her brow furrowed and her eyes squeezed tightly shut. White fog covers her body, thick and glistening, and fragile threads of deep red twist through it like a frayed web. Her mouth is moving, though, as are her hands. She's gnashing her teeth while she claws at the sheets, at her checkered hospital gown, at her skin. Already she's got bloody scrapes down her cheek from her own fingernails.

And all the while, she's only making that kitten-like, mewling sound.

My mouth opens to call for the nurse.

The girl's eyes fly wide. Land on me. She lunges from the bed like a wild animal, her blue-painted nails sinking into my shoulders and her face contorted into a desperate cry. The fog strikes at the same moment, covering my body, surrounding us both, and it's pouring into me.

Memory comes with it. The club. The dancing. The white mist everywhere, twisting over me, sinking into my skin.

And the way I'd run from it. The way I can't escape now.

I gasp. It feels good. Like adrenaline and euphoria and, oh God, lust. The red threads are like stinging counterpoints, painful amid the pleasure, but they're almost lost in the flood of sensation. My body tingles, flashing hot and burning from one heartbeat to the next, and I choke on a cry, overwhelmed. But that's not all of it. Not everything I'm feeling.

There's something wrong—with her, obviously, but more than that. In my head, I can feel it somehow. Something has gone wrong inside her. She…

I take a strangled breath, and in my mind, I try to push the mist back. Push it out of me. *Away* from me.

Into her.

The girl's blue eyes widen. The rabid craze in them turns to shock. Fear, like a small child waking from a nightmare. Her hands on my shoulders still clutch me, but it's not the same. Not clawing. Just hanging on like she needs me. Like I'm the only thing keeping her standing.

But only for a moment. Her knees buckle. I grab her, pushing her back toward the bed before she can fall to the ground. In a heap, she collapses onto the tangle of sheets.

I stare at her, my heart galloping beneath my ribs and my whole body shaking.

"What are you *doing*?"

I jump, my eyes snapping to the doorway at the harsh whisper.

He's standing there. The guy from the club. From the street. A matte-black jacket covers him now, and if not for the moonlight streaming through the window on the other side of the room, he'd disappear into the thick shadows entirely.

But he's here. Like he was on the street, here. Appearing where he couldn't be, on the seventh floor of a building that's mostly shut down for the night. Terrified, I back away.

Or try to.

My legs won't hold me. The adrenaline of the past moments has shot all my reserves of energy. I crumple back against the pale green curtain and hear the rings clatter on the metal pole overhead.

He's at my side in an instant, his strong hands catching me before I can fall farther.

Breathing suddenly becomes distinctly optional.

"You're hurt," he hisses. "You need your strength. Why are you—"

He cuts off when he catches sight of the dark-haired girl on the bed, and his face goes still. It lasts only a heartbeat, though. He turns back to me, and the odd expression is gone.

"Come on," he says rather than continue berating me.

His grip adjusts on me, one arm sliding around my back while the other takes my legs, and he lifts me effortlessly. Instinctively, my arms wrap around his neck, hanging on tight while he carries me to the hospital bed.

And I can't breathe. I *so* can't breathe. Part of me—the sane, rational, smart-Caitlin part of me—wants to scream bloody murder for the nurse. Because he was there, right when I noticed the fog for the first time, right when I realized what was happening to me. It could be his fault for all I know.

But the rest of me isn't listening. The rest of me is locked on him. On the sensation of his jacket against my bare legs, the fabric warmed by his body. On the way I can feel his muscles moving in his chest when he turns with me in his arms. I bite my lip, all manner of urges and thoughts flying through my head.

Gently, he lowers me to the hospital bed. His arms leave me, and he sinks down, folding into the chair at my bedside with fluid ease. He's comfortable in his body, I can tell. More comfortable than anyone I've ever seen. Moonlight touches his skin and shoulders with silver, though much of his face is hidden in the shadow the light casts.

But his eyes are on me. I can see them, barely, in the darkness. They make it difficult to think.

"Who are you?" I whisper.

He regards me for a moment. "Amar Okoro. You?"

"Caitlin Faire. Or Cait, really. Just Cait." I'm babbling,

but I can't help it. I can't stop staring at him. He hasn't stopped watching me.

"What House are you with?" he asks.

"House?"

He pauses. His gaze flicks to the girl on the other bed and then back. "Neutral?" He offers the question like he doubts its likelihood. Like this makes any sense at all.

I shake my head slowly, not taking my eyes from him. "I'm not… I don't know what you're…" I try to regroup. "What is this? Did you do this to me?"

"Do… what?"

"The fog thing. The—" I motion to the girl. I don't know how to describe it. I feel half-mad already, and his guarded look isn't helping. "Did you do that? Are you why I'm suddenly *seeing* things and feeling this…"

He's watching me like he can't figure out what to make of me. Like he thought I was one thing, but now I'm turning into something completely different.

Something that might bite.

"I'm not sure what you're talking about," he replies carefully.

I start trembling, hard, and some part of me wants to cry. I know what I saw. At least, what I *think* I saw. He'd absorbed the fog too. Not only that, he'd looked like he knew *exactly* what he was doing the whole time.

His expression shifts again. The changes are minute, always so minute, and I get the impression that closed books are more forthcoming than he's accustomed to being. But his gaze flickers over me like he's reconsidering something all the same. "I didn't do that," he amends.

I wait, not sure I believe him.

"But you've never had that happen before," he continues, gingerly and not at all like a question. More like he's picking the words the way someone tests their path across a potentially frozen lake.

I bite back an incredulous sound and shake my head again, still watching him.

"Your parent didn't explain this to you?"

Singular, not plural. "Parent?" I repeat carefully.

His eyes narrow like he's evaluating something, and I can't tell what. Me, maybe.

The squeak of tennis shoes on tile comes from the hallway. My gaze darts toward it. The nurse.

Amar is out of the chair in a heartbeat, and he strides past me fast. My mouth moves, words failing to come, and I don't even know what they would have been. A request for him to stop? To explain what the hell he'd meant?

He slips out the door.

My body moves of its own accord. I shove up from the bed and stagger across the room as quickly as my legs will carry me. My hands catch on the cold doorframe, and I take a breath to call out to him.

The words die unspoken. The nurse is several doors farther down the hallway, a cart beside her with a tray of Dixie cups and pills on top. Lowered lights create dim patches of illumination amid the shadows in the long hall.

And otherwise, there's nothing. No closing doors, no gorgeous-but-unsettling guy walking away, and no sign the nurse has seen anyone at all. At the end of the long corridor, the stairwell door is still, and the elevator doors are as well.

Amar is gone.

3

One week later, I'm more convinced than ever that Amar has done something to me.

I feel like a ping-pong ball ricocheting between extremes. I can't sleep. I'm exhausted. I can barely eat. I'm starving.

And I'm shaky all the time.

I bundle the sleeves of my sweater into my fists and try to make it down the steps and out the front door before my stepmother returns and realizes I've come by the house.

"And just what do you think you're doing?"

I freeze, my stomach sinking, and I don't turn around. I thought Arlene wasn't here. That she'd gone out to breakfast with her friends. I always try to time my visits for that, to see Dad when she's not at the house. It's easier that way.

But I look like hell, and that's without the bruises from a week ago. My eyes are sunken pits, underscored by purple rings like I got confused about where the dark eye shadow was supposed to go. My lips look as if I've painted them with talcum powder. Corpses have more life to their appearance right now.

She knows I was hit by a car, knows I've been out of class for a week as a result, but I also know her. She'll accuse me of being on drugs, purely based on what I look like.

I'd rather face a rabid mongoose than deal with *that*.

"Nothing," I manage, continuing down the stairs with the careful movements of someone who's inching away from an attack dog. "I just stopped to check on—"

"You know the rules. You call first. You clear it with me. You don't just 'drop by.'" She makes a disgusted noise. "I know why you're here. You want him to give you money again, don't you? Well, forget it. You have to grow up sometime, Caitlin."

I tremble, pointless rage boiling in the pit of my stomach. I've held a job since I was fourteen, and I haven't asked for a dime, barring when some asshole pulled a hit-and-run on my car two years ago and insurance wouldn't cover all the repairs.

Not that she's ever going to let me forget it. I'm a leech. The one she and my father shouldn't have been forced to take care of.

I bolt down the rest of the stairs.

"Don't think I'm letting you get away with—"

I slam the door on her words. My shoes thud on the porch steps as I run toward my car.

She doesn't follow. I thank God for small miracles while I start the engine and then put the gearshift into reverse.

My gaze catches on the bedroom window on the second floor. It's closed, as usual. The light hurts Dad's eyes. But just for a moment, I pretend I see a crack between the curtains. I let myself think he's looking down at me.

Even if I know it can't be true.

My hand shakes as I tug the gearshift into drive and take off down the street.

It wasn't till I was four years old that the symptoms started, but my stepmom blames them on me all the same. Or, really, on my biological mother. Even if the doctors have never found the slightest indication Dad's trouble stems from some sexually transmitted infection, Arlene's convinced my mother is responsible.

Dad's one night of infidelity. He'd been out at a bar, cooling off after a fight with Arlene, and that's when he met her. My mother. Or, as Arlene calls her, that "bar-crawling whore."

He barely even remembers it. Her. She was a brunette. Hazel eyes like mine. Name he can't recall. She was gone when he woke up in her hotel room the next morning, and for better or worse, he kept quiet about what he'd done— that is until I showed up, dumped on his doorstep in a bassinet nine months later.

She left a note, at least. Explained that she couldn't keep me and that, as the one who hopefully would be my caretaker, she figured he should have the right to name me. It was nice. Neat.

Cold.

Arlene went postal. Thought some "crack whore" was making up stories. And Dad… he could have lied. Taken me to the nearest police station or hospital and just left me. But he didn't. He insisted they keep me instead. He came clean to his wife, explained what had happened, and swore I was his responsibility.

He was a good man, my dad. Still is… mostly.

My hands flex on the steering wheel. It started with muscle weakness. Progressed from there to tremors and then fainting spells. He's been bedridden for the better part of eight years now, and the doctors don't have a clue what is wrong. He's undergone every test known to God or man and taken every immune-boosting concoction I can find—and hide from Arlene—for him. It doesn't matter. He stays sick all the same.

So Arlene blames me and my invisible, nameless mom. Apparently, it's easier that way.

Sometimes I think that, even if she *had* somehow learned that Dad cheated on her, she would have gone on like the little "indiscretion" never happened. She would have carried on like they were just this perfect family: her, my dad, and their twin daughters, Kelly and Bethany— both of whom were younger than me, most likely born to make up for me, and well on their way to respectable college programs where they're certain to meet rich husbands. Arlene would have her meetings with the local Rotary Club, her yappy little Pomeranian named Pixie, and her white picket fence around her two-story blue colonial. Everything would have been flawless.

But I'm here. I'm the fly in the milk, the constant reminder of what happened that night. And I won't move away, not when he's so sick, and I come back to see him even when she's made it clear I'm not welcome. I have to. He's my dad. Sure, he's always missed most of what Arlene says, what she does. She hides it. Hell, *I* hide it. Arlene would just scream or cry or call me a liar, and then he'd get upset.

He's weak enough. He doesn't need anything else stressing his health.

But regardless, he's the only real family I have. And he

swears I'll always be welcome. He always tells me, this deep concern in his watery blue eyes, that there's a place for me there. Like I'm the one—not her—who is keeping me away.

While I just fear the day he dies.

I pull into a parallel parking spot several blocks from my first class. The area is fairly empty for campus, with almost no students this far out, but I don't bother trying to find anything closer. I know from past experience that, by the time I'm done driving around in circles, looking for a spot near the main quad, I could have already walked the whole way to class.

My legs quiver beneath me when I climb from my sky-blue box of a car. It occurs to me that the same thing that happened to Dad might be happening to me. Like, maybe this isn't Amar. Maybe it's genetic.

I shut the door harder than necessary, as if to trap the idea in the car.

It makes more sense than people emitting mist that slipped into my body, though.

I shove that thought down as well. My jaw clenches while I feed quarters into the meter and then stalk toward class. I ignore the aching in my bones and the burning in my muscles. It's getting worse, that pain. Every passing day, the raw feeling like my body is tearing itself apart from the inside out just gets stronger. I don't know why. What's changed.

But it hurts.

My hands grip the straps of my backpack against my shoulders. My chest heaves with the effort of breathing. I lock my eyes on the sidewalk as if to ground myself and keep from giving in to the nausea churning in my stomach.

This can't be the same thing that happened to Dad. He

never said a word about fog, about absorbing it, about anything. Hell, half the time he just jokes that he has a cold and he'll get over it soon.

Maybe Amar poisoned me.

I swallow hard and risk a glance up, checking how much farther I have till I reach my building.

My steps falter.

The sidewalks this close to the quad are crowded, even for late morning. Students are everywhere: walking, hanging out, waiting for buses, or rushing to their next class. Wisps of fog drift through the air around them. A bit here, a bit there, none of it as dense as what had been at the club, but all of it misty and sparkling.

And suddenly, I'm shaking. I can't stop. I feel so strange, so desperate, like a junkie who's gone too long without a hit. I want to cry, or maybe just run like hell, but I can't make my feet move. I'm fairly certain my mouth is open, panting.

What's wrong with me?

I tear my gaze away, but it only locks on some guy nearby. He's big. Muscular. Probably a football player or a wannabe. He's got a tousled mess of brown hair that looks as if he's decided he's too cool to brush it, and he's lounging against a low stone wall that separates the library from the street. Four of his friends are around him. They're ogling the girls walking by like they're rating what they see.

Fog pours off him like condensation from an icy beer bottle.

He sees me watching him, and he grins.

It's enough.

My body moves of its own accord. I can't stop it. I don't even know what I'm doing. But suddenly, I'm striding over there, drawn to him as if by gravity, aiming for him like an arrow seeking a target.

His grin turns to a smirk. I can tell he's not evaluating me like the other girls. I don't look like much, after all. Old jeans. Cable-knit sweater. Ragged backpack I bought three years ago and haven't wanted to spend the money to replace. He nudges one of his friends, everything in his demeanor making it clear he thinks some crazy chick is about to protest what they've been doing.

"Hey there," he greets me, dry amusement in his voice.

"Hey," I reply, and then I'm past his friends and right up in front of him.

His eyes go wide, his amusement growing while he eyes me up and down. My heart is slamming against my ribs. My gaze sweeps over him hungrily. My hand comes up, and my fingers run down his jacket.

Mist slips into my skin, and oh God, it feels like heaven.

"Whoa," one of his friends scoffs. "What the—"

I don't think. Don't plan. Between one second and the next, I move forward, kissing him.

It's like water in the desert. Like rain on a dying plant. The pain in my body fades, and there's just peace. Pleasure. A tingling spreading through me like itty-bitty Christmas lights coming on throughout my veins.

Holy shit. And I thought touching his chest was nice…

I pull back, staring into his wide, vaguely poleaxed blue eyes. I want more of that. *Need* more.

I have no idea what I'm doing.

The thought flits through my head: this isn't me. This isn't even *close* to me. I'm withdrawn around guys. Careful not to get involved. I've had two not-quite-boyfriends in the history of ever, and Arlene made my life hell over it both times.

I'll do anything to keep from proving her right with all her accusations about apples not falling far from trees.

But right now, I don't care. I *can't* care. My fingers fist around the front of his jacket, drawing him with me while I retreat from his friends.

"Dude, are you crazy?" his friend protests when he comes with me.

The guy just grins like he's won the lottery.

I ignore them, my gaze raking across the crowds around me. I need… I don't know what I need.

"Why don't you and me go someplace private, eh?" He nods toward the nearest building. Physics Department, maybe.

How ironic.

I head for the door.

"Hey, now." He pries my fingers from his jacket. "No need to damage anything. I'm coming."

He shifts my grip from his coat to his hand, and his skin sends shivers racing through me. The steps fall behind us, then the door. The marble-floored hall is choked with people, and for a moment, I'm disoriented. He tugs on my hand, though, heading toward a narrow doorway. The men's room. It's surprisingly empty for the time of day, and he takes advantage of that fact immediately, flipping the lock on the door the moment it's closed behind us.

The stench of industrial cleaners, old mildew, and smelly guys burns my nostrils. Urinals and open stalls wait to my left while porcelain sinks and scuffed mirrors are on the right. Ahead, there are windows of frosted glass that reach up to the high ceiling and a half-wall of chipped marble that ends with a wide ledge below them.

He spins me around, and then his lips are on mine. His hands push my backpack from my shoulders; I hear it thud to the floor and feel him move when he kicks it aside. His tongue shoves into my mouth. I taste beef jerky, maybe some coffee.

It's disgusting.

It's barely a footnote in what's happening.

Mist is pouring into me like a torrent, a thousand times stronger than it had been at the club. I can feel it stealing the remnants of the shakiness and the pain. I can feel it surging through me like it's turning on the lights in my whole world. I'm having trouble thinking, though. The room is blurring. Condensing. Coming down to nothing but the glittery exhilaration racing through my veins. I barely notice his mouth devouring mine or the way his rank breath is hot against my face. I barely notice anything. Irrational, inexplicable *ecstasy* is rushing through me, and so what if I don't even know this guy? I need this. I need—

His hands return to my body, and he startles me when he moves me backward, his mouth never leaving mine. We stumble up against the wall on the far side of the room, and he presses to me, the hardness of his crotch bulging against my hip. Cold marble chills my back when his hand shoves under my sweater and pushes the knit fabric up. His fingers climb fast to my bra and unhook it with a swift maneuver. I don't try to stop him. I can barely think the words. His sweaty palm takes my breast, clutching it, squeezing down hard, and out of nowhere, wet heat flares between my legs. His mouth breaks from mine as he tries to catch his breath, and he looks down while his other hand works on unfastening the closure of my jeans.

I tilt my head back, a tingling sensation rushing

through my body as suddenly, I realize what comes next. What *has* to come next.

But this is madness. This is utter *insanity*. I've spent my whole life determined not to let Arlene's insults be right, and now I'm going to let some stranger take my virginity in a public restroom? What the hell is wrong with—

His fingers slip from my jeans, thudding against my hip before attempting to return again. I look down, confused.

He's gasping like he can't get enough air. His eyes are wide, staring unseeing at the wall, and though his hands still fumble at me, his mouth gapes open like a beached fish. Even if he looks like he's a heartbeat from bliss, his skin is colorless. I can see purple veins throbbing in his temples and neck.

The sight hits me like cold water, spreading cracks through my exhilaration. I stumble away from him.

He starts to fall. His hands grasp at the wall like the slick marble can support him, and then he's on his knees. Tumbling to his side. Lying on the floor and still reaching toward me, an expression on his face like he's desperate for me to keep touching him.

Oh God, what have I done?

Mist still connects us. Thick ropes of it, pouring from him into my body.

A shriek escapes me. Instinctively, I retreat while my hands swipe at the fog, trying to break its hold. My heels catch my backpack. I slam down onto my ass on the cold floor.

The pain shatters the last traces of exhilaration dulling my thoughts and takes the ropes of fog with it. And then there's just horror. He's still on the ground. His movements are weaker, although his skin looks better. He's gasping, but more like he's been running a marathon than suffocating in the open air.

I start shaking. What the… what the…

My body moves before my brain catches up. My hands snag my backpack from the ground, and my legs carry me, slamming me up against the door. I struggle with the lock. A panicked noise leaves me when I tear the door open and students are everywhere, blocking the exit to the street.

I don't think. I just take off in the opposite direction.

People shout. I can hear them yelling when I shove past, but their faces blur. Everything blurs. They're going to find him at any moment.

Should I call the cops first? Tell someone he's there? And claim… what? His friends will vouch that I came onto him, not the other way around. And now he's on the floor. He's—

Oh God, what if he dies?

I round the corner, racing blindly for an escape, and I slam headlong into a tall, dark-skinned wall.

Amar catches me as I stagger back from him, gaping. He's here.

Oh, sweet God, of *course* he's here.

I want to scream.

Shouts come from farther down the hall at my back. Different shouts. Somebody's found the guy on the bathroom floor.

Amar takes one look from me to the hallway, and then he turns, his hand still holding me. He strides toward the bright square of sunlight that is the door, and I stumble after him, tugged along by his vice-like grip on my arm.

People clear from his path like a parting sea. Light glares in my eyes when he pushes past the door and continues down the stairs toward the quad. Blinking fast, I glance around.

We're only getting a few stares. Even those fall behind us when we reach the sidewalk and he shifts his grip, pulling me close to his side as if we're arm-in-arm like a couple.

But he doesn't stop moving. He marches past the library, past everything. It's like he's going to walk right off campus.

Sirens howl in the distance behind us. New spikes of terror shoot through me.

"What..." I can't form words, and my breaths are ragged gasps. Amar glances down at the sound of my voice, though, and then tosses a look behind us. Wide-eyed, I follow his gaze. It almost seems like he's checking to see if anyone's trailing us.

He appears to accept whatever he finds, though. His steps divert toward a low wall beside a building I don't recognize. The area around us is fairly deserted now that classes have started and the quad's long gone. Distant traffic and those horrible sirens are the only sounds.

"Sit," he orders, half-pushing me toward the wall. I collapse onto it, my palms bracing me on the rough stone. Never looking away from me, he slings his bag around and unzips it before tugging out a bottle of water. "Drink."

He pushes the bottle into my grip, still watching my face. I fumble open the cap and gulp down a mouthful. I can't take my eyes from him.

His brow rises slightly. "Better?"

"What did you do to me?" I whisper, the words nearly a sob.

He scowls. "I didn't do anything." His gaze drops

away briefly, and after a moment, his apparent irritation fades. He takes a seat beside me with a sigh.

I shift away from him ever so slightly. I can tell he notices from the way his jaw tightens, but he doesn't say a word.

I can't take the silence. "What… what are… what am…"

His head turns. His dark eyes meet mine. "Demon."

My jaw trembles. I bite my lip. Hard.

"But, given how you haven't…" He hesitates, revising. "How this hasn't happened to you till now… I'm guessing you're half. Like me."

My brows inch upward.

"It's as good as whole, though. Your dad, your mom, one of them was this. And we are what they are. We grow up human, but eventually… our natures take over." Amar pauses. "It just usually starts a whole lot earlier than, well —" He nods toward me.

I'm shivering. My whole body, it's just quaking like there's a gyroscope whirling out of control in my insides. My head shakes back and forth of its own accord. I want to argue with him. Laugh. Do anything to deny what he's said.

But how else do I explain what happened?

The thought makes my stomach churn, and I clamp my lips shut, afraid for a moment that all the water will come rushing back up my throat. This can't be happening. It can't… it can't be…

"How do I stop it?" My voice is a rasp.

"Stop…?"

"*This*. The…" I can't make myself say the word. "The *thing*. What's happening to me. How do I… how can I…" I rub my palm over my thigh hard, trying to keep from panicking. "This started somehow. So how do I make it stop?"

He's silent for a moment. "You can't."

A harsh breath leaves me, and I bolt up from the stone wall, though my shaky legs can't carry me more than a few steps before the ground wobbles. "No. No, there *has* to be a way to… to make this not…" I turn back to face him. "I don't have to stay like this. I won't."

He's watching me like he's never quite seen anything like me before in his life. "Like what?"

"*This*! A monster who… who *hurts* people."

The words blurt from me, my voice high and just shy of a frantic shriek, and for a heartbeat, I tense, suddenly worried he's going to lash out. To get angry or disgusted with me because I basically just insulted him, considering he said he was like this too.

But he doesn't do that. He just… blinks. His brow draws down a bit, and that curiosity comes back into his eyes, except it's different than the "might bite" look he gave me at the hospital. Not wary. More… surprised. Intrigued, maybe, or something I can't even find a word for, because anything soft or gentle doesn't seem to fit this guy.

But it's definitely curious, and it's not the same.

"Okay," he says. "You… you don't have to be a monster. Or hurt people."

I study him distrustfully.

"What you are, though." He wets his lips, seeming to search for words. "Or who your parent was, or what that means for you…" A grimace crosses his face. "It's not really something you can change."

I shift my weight like I can escape the words because

surely he has to be wrong. Maybe *he* just doesn't want to change. Maybe—

"Trust me, if I could—" He cuts off, his grimace turning bitter. "If there was a way…" He exhales. "But there's not. There's just… not. And that *doesn't* make you a monster."

His eyes find mine. After a second, he nods toward the stone wall again.

I bite my lip and then walk over and sit down.

"You're not some evil creature," he says. "Demon is simply a… a catchall description for us. It's what others have labeled us, not what we have to consider ourselves."

"What others?" I whisper.

"Priests. Shamans. Professors."

There's the barest note of humor in his voice on the final word, and a smile pulls at the corner of his lip. I stare at him.

"Like researchers and academics," he amends, burying the expression and tone quickly, like he's not used to letting someone know that he finds anything amusing. "There are many names for us, all sorts of things we've been mistaken for or accused of being over the centuries. The Zulu have Tikoloshe, the Chileans have Trauco. There's qarinah, Ardat Lili, or Irdu Lili. Plenty of others. None of them are exactly the same as us, but the closest ones you might recognize…"

I can't breathe. My brain is spinning. And he's watching me like he's weighing whether I can handle the rest of the sentence. "What?" I ask.

"Succubi and incubi."

The ground feels like it's shifting. My fingers tighten on the rough stone of the wall.

"You're *not evil*, Cait," he repeats.

I manage to move my head in something approximating a nod. There's no other option. It's that or throw up.

"You're just… different."

A harsh laugh escapes me. That has to be the understatement of my *life*.

He sighs.

"So, what is it?" I ask him. "The… that mist thing. Y-you saw it. I mean, in the club, I saw you…"

He shrugs. "Sexual energy, more or less. When a human is aroused or attracted to someone sexually, we can see it. And, you know, feed off it."

I'm back to staring at him again.

"It's necessary for us. It's not evil either. Feeding like that, it helps us. It makes us what we are. I don't know how you survived for this long without needing that, but you still used up a lot of your energy when you were hit by that car. And then to help that Protected at the hospital—"

"That what?"

He frowns like he got ahead of himself. "It's complicated. Never mind. The point is, your injuries would have been a lot worse if you were human. You kept yourself alive, but you must have drained yourself in doing that, and I'm guessing you haven't replenished any energy since." His dark eyes watch me intently, something knowing in them. Something I'd swear to God was sympathetic. "It had to feel like you were falling apart."

I scoff, but I can't hold his gaze. Falling apart wasn't the half of it.

And as for the rest of what he's said…

I bottle the information up fast. I can't think about that right now. "So you were, what? Following me? Back there, or at the hospital, or at the club, you were just—"

Straightening, he draws a breath like he's making himself refocus—though God knows what distracted him—and he turns his attention to the road. "I saw you run out at Temptation, and I was concerned," he says. "You seemed fine, like you were having a good time, and then you took off. I thought something might have happened that I should know about."

"Like what?"

He pauses, and it's not like before. Not just weighing my responses. Darker than that and a hell of a lot more closed off. "It doesn't matter. I misread the situation. But as for later at the hospital… you panicked when you spotted me on the street, and that seemed odd because I thought you knew what you are. What *we* are. And then you got hit by a car. I wanted to find out what was going on and if you were all right."

My fingers adjust around the water bottle. The plastic label crinkles beneath my grip. "And today?"

Amar hesitates. "Coincidence, actually. I was just coming from class. Quantum Physics lab."

I blink.

"What?" he asks.

I drop my gaze away, shaking my head. I don't know how to answer, or really what the question would have been. It just seems so… normal. Really intelligent, obviously, which is hot, but… still. Normal.

And I almost killed someone in the men's room. Because I'm a… because my mother was most likely a…

He nudges the bottle like he can see me starting to freak again. I notice how he's careful not to let his hand touch mine. "Drink," he says.

On autopilot, I swallow another mouthful, not taking my gaze from the ground. The water helps.

"Where were you headed?" he asks. "Before..."

"Computer Science. Data structures class."

From the corner of my eye, I see his eyebrow twitch upward, that odd curiosity flickering back into his expression. "Really?" he asks, a surprised note in his voice.

"What?"

"Nothing. It's just... not quite what I would've expected."

"What'd you expect?"

He's quiet for a second, and then a soft chuckle leaves him. "I honestly don't know."

I'm not quite sure what to say to that. I get that I'm a nerd, but I don't care. Computers are easier than people. They're straightforward—for the most part, anyway. Arlene hates it; swears I'll only meet losers who are certain to move into their mothers' basements when school is over —and thus, I'll come crawling to her for money—but that doesn't matter. Guys aren't the point. And I wouldn't ask her for anything if my life depended on it.

I realize my mind is babbling again, but it's okay. Talking about classes is ordinary and grounding. I glance up at Amar, and something in his expression makes it seem like that was his intention the whole time—though now I'd swear he almost looks interested in me too.

My chest does a weird, fluttering thing, and I feel my cheeks heat up. "Physics, huh?" I manage.

Amar nods. "I graduate next year. You?"

"Probably. You thinking grad school?"

"Yeah."

"Yeah."

The conversation stutters into silence.

"What happened back there?" he asks quietly.

I tremble. I don't want to respond.

I don't have a choice. He's the only one with answers here. "A-a guy. I, um…"

"You have sex with him?"

I gawp at him. I can't believe he just asked that—and so casually too. Like I just bumped into the guy in the hallway or something. I mean, I barely even *know* Amar. Sure, at least I know his *name*, which is a damn sight better than the stranger I'd been about to let into my pants, but that doesn't equal wanting to talk about—

"In the men's bathroom?" I bluster to cover how intensely uncomfortable I am.

Amar just looks at me. "You let yourself get desperate enough, anything'll do."

I'm dumbstruck by the solemnity in his eyes. "Just kissing," I manage.

"And what happened?"

"He fell. He was all pale and shaking, and I—"

"You were draining him too fast."

It's hard to even blink. He grimaces at my expression.

"When you're feeding like that, it—" His grimace deepens, and for the first time, he looks uncomfortable too. "It's a drug for them. Humans. The effect we have on them— the effect of what we're *doing* to them—is overwhelming. They'll pour out everything they have to you, if you let them, even if it costs them their life. So you have to control it. Let it take time. Let them…"

"Get off on it?" I fill in, guessing what he's going to say. "Finish?"

"Yeah. And if you're careful, you won't hurt anybody."

My mouth moves, but I can't find words. I'm having the most insane conversation of my life.

"Will he die?" I blurt.

Amar hesitates. I hate it. I read everything horrible into it and feel like throwing up all over again.

"When you stopped," he asks, "what happened? How did he look?"

I choke down a breath. "B-better, I think. His skin wasn't so pale, and his breathing was, you know, not as bad." I give a helpless shrug.

"He should probably be okay, then."

I watch him, feeling a bit like a kid desperate to have someone help her keep believing in Santa Claus. I mean, I could have killed someone today. Actually, honestly *murdered* somebody.

Because I'm a demon.

"Really, Cait. It's when they get worse after you stop that's bad."

I swallow hard. I know he's trying to be reassuring. It's kind of nice.

It just doesn't change much.

My cell phone buzzes.

I nearly jump out of my skin. My hands shaking, I fish the phone out of my pocket. It's a text from Ruby.

For a moment, I just stare at it, feeling like I'm looking at another world. Reality, which has nothing to do with this bizarre place I've ended up. I'm Alice, talking over some nightmare Wonderland with the Cheshire Cat. With the Caterpillar. Something.

It's a far cry from Ruby and all that I thought was real when I woke up this morning.

"Everything okay?" Amar asks.

"Y-yeah. My friend. We're supposed to meet for lunch after class."

He nods. I tuck the phone and the water bottle into my bag, and then push to my feet, willing my legs to hold me.

I only shake a little bit.

My eyes skirting around, I hoist my backpack higher on my shoulders. "So, um, now what?"

"You probably got a fair amount of energy from him, so you should be all right for a little while. The craving is going to come back, though, so just be—"

"Will I see you again? On purpose, I mean. Not just, like, out of nowhere?"

My heart is pounding, and the way he pauses makes it worse. I have no idea what he thinks of me, but I can't deny that I'm attracted to him. He's gorgeous. Intelligent. He's the kind of guy I'd be hella interested in under different circumstances, and when you add in that he basically saved my ass today… God, it's a heady combination. Plus, he only followed me to the hospital because he was curious about me and because he wanted to know if I was all right. To top it all off, he has answers about this madness.

I want to see him again. No, scratch that. I *need* to.

But his pause just doesn't end, and in only a few moments, I feel like a moron. His expression is becoming like Fort Knox, all locked up and inaccessible as hell. I'd swear he seems to be drawing away from me, even if he hasn't moved a muscle.

He's got to be searching for a way to tell me no.

"Okay, well…" I turn to go. "Thanks for the talk, anyway. And the water. I'll, uh, see you if I see you."

I take off, wincing at the idiotic statement. My head tucked down and my hands clutching the straps of my backpack, I stride away as fast as my legs will carry me and try to ignore the way he doesn't even say goodbye.

4

I CIRCLE WIDE OF THE QUAD ON MY WAY TO MEET RUBY, JUST
in case. The sirens faded a while ago, and that guy's
friends are probably staying near their buddy, but it still
pays to be careful.

I wonder if the cops have a way to track me. I wonder
if they'll try. No one died, after all. Maybe it'll be okay.

Maybe his friends will come looking for me.

By the time I reach the restaurant, I'm a jittery mess.
My stomach is twisting into so many pretzels that it's
probably breaking the laws of physics. Even the rich aroma
of Indian food can't fix it. I duck past the door and spend a
moment in the entryway, trying to let go of the fight-or-
flight panic that makes me feel like I'm being chased.

Even if no one has given me a second glance this whole
time.

I take a deep breath and make myself continue inside.
Goa Cafe has been our favorite spot for lunch since Ruby
and I started college. It's two-stories high, with the second
floor overlooking the first, and tall windows that stretch

up the entirety of the front wall. One corner is occupied by a rocky fountain with a beautiful statue of Ganesh on top, while another is taken up by easy chairs and low tables for studying. The ordering counter is on the far side of the first floor, with stanchions and ropes cordoning off plenty of space for the lines that usually form, and round tables crowd the rest of the room, all of their tops painted with richly colored, abstract designs. Between the comfort and the food, it's basically the perfect place to hang out and relax, and we take every chance we can get to come here.

It barely calms me today.

My fingers adjust nervously on my backpack while I walk deeper into the restaurant. Most people are in classes still, so the place hasn't filled up as much as it will once the lunch crowd arrives. I take the opportunity to grab an empty table while I wait for Ruby.

Minutes crawl by. I'm twitching every time the door opens or someone comes close to my table.

Ruby walks past the windows, scanning the restaurant. She's got her black hair pulled back in a messy ponytail, and she's wearing a green, waist-length jacket that might be designer, though I'm not sure. She catches sight of me and waves.

She's not alone.

My brow twitches down. She's talking with a dark-haired guy, but I've never seen him before. He's attractive, almost male-model attractive, even if he's simply wearing a t-shirt, coat, and jeans. He reaches around her to take the door and holds it open while she smiles and laughs.

"Hey!" she calls to me cheerily. They cross the restaurant to the table. "I thought it'd take you longer to get here."

"Class let out early."

My eyes dart from her to the guy as I speak. She grins at the sight.

"This is Kyle." She motions to him, and I blink when I realize she's blushing.

Ruby. Blushing. I don't think she's blushed in her life.

"Hey," he says. "You must be Cait."

Even his voice is smooth. Charming. Somehow, it conveys utter nonchalance while also making it seem like I'm the only one he sees in the room.

I swallow hard at the sound. "Nice to meet you." I glance back to Ruby. "So, um—"

"We ran into each other outside my last class. He's in Political Science too. Hoping to go to Harvard Law."

My eyebrows rise, making it clear I'm suitably impressed. "Wow. That's great. Just like you, huh?"

Ruby grins. "I know, right?"

She turns the expression on Kyle, who just shrugs. "Small world, eh? You want me to grab food?"

Her grin gets wider. "That'd be awesome. Thanks."

"You ordering anything?" he asks me.

I shake my head. "Not hungry."

Ruby's focus is on me instantly. "Seriously?"

"Yeah." I'm not exactly lying. My stomach is still a mess. I probably couldn't eat anything if I tried.

Her brow furrows, but Kyle just nods. "Back in a minute."

He threads past the tables while Ruby sinks into the chair opposite me, an intent expression on her face. "You sure you're okay?"

"Yeah."

She doesn't appear convinced, but my glance to Kyle distracts her. A smile tugs at her lip immediately. "Like *damn*, right?"

"And then some," I agree, but it's hard to get my heart behind the words. Something feels off here, and I can't put my finger on it. Ruby is beautiful. People in outer space can probably see that Ruby is beautiful. She was one of the most popular girls in our high school, and it was just a freak twist of fate and her own good nature that ended us up as friends. It makes sense someone who looks like Kyle would be interested in her.

But something about this is still bothering me, and I have no idea why.

"So'd you see that ambulance today?"

I flinch. "What?"

"I was getting updates on my phone like crazy. A guy collapsed in the building next door to yours. People called 911, ambulance showed up, the whole deal. You didn't see that?"

I choke down a breath. "Oh, uh, no. I just…" I can't think of anything to say.

She studies me. "You sure you're all right?"

"Totally." I hesitate. "You hear if the guy was okay?"

"I don't know. They took him to the hospital, but from what I heard, he was conscious when they did, so…" She shrugs.

I nod. She's still studying me. I scramble to think of something to distract her.

Kyle saves me. "Food should be ready in a few minutes," he says as he comes back to the table. He sinks into a chair beside Ruby, and smiles when she looks his way.

"Thanks," she says.

"No problem." He turns his smile on me. "So, Cait, Ruby tells me you two are locals."

It's difficult to look away from his green eyes. "Yeah."

"Well, sort of," Ruby clarifies. "My family moved to Arizona when I started college, so I'm only part local now, I guess you could say. Cait's family is still in town, though. Where are you from?"

"Oh, here, there. Probably everywhere." Kyle grins. It's like he never stops. "Dad's a business consultant. We moved a lot for his work."

I don't take my eyes from him while Ruby makes a comment about corporate versions of military brats and Kyle laughs. Everything seems fine. Totally normal and fine.

That doesn't do jack shit for the weird, all-hands-on-deck feeling crawling up my spine as if some predator is sneaking between the restaurant tables, just beyond the corner of my eye.

"It wasn't so bad," Kyle continues. "I have a pretty big family, so you know, it's not like you get *lonely* or anything."

Ruby chuckles. "Lonely, no. *Annoyed* on the other hand…"

He gives her a curious look.

"Three younger brothers and two younger sisters," she explains. "Bathroom time was a *nightmare*, growing up."

His grin returns. "Oh, I know all about that. What about you, Cait? You have a good-sized family around you?"

I don't know why I hesitate. It's a simple enough question.

Nothing feels simple right now.

"Not like Ruby's," I say.

His curious expression comes back, inviting me to go on.

Food shows up, sparing me, and I practically tremble with relief at the sight. The cafe owner, Pradeep, recognizes us, and we exchange a few pleasantries about the day while he delivers food for the others and water for me, though he has to hurry away again when a line starts to form at the counter.

My stomach churns at the aroma of the food regardless of the fact that, normally, I love the dishes here. I swallow hard and look to the window, hoping my apparent distraction will make Kyle drop the family subject. Every subject, for that matter.

"Your family's not like Ruby's, huh?" Kyle comments to me.

My twisting stomach sinks. So much for that. "No."

A pause follows the words, practically begging me to continue. I pick up my glass, taking a sip of water rather than fill the quiet.

"So," Ruby begins, her tone hinting that she thinks I'm being rude. "What about that Harvard application, huh? Pretty crazy, right?"

"*Oh* yeah," Kyle agrees.

They carry on without me, talking about their applications, their general level of stress about the school, and the dreaded LSATs. At the last, Kyle's eyebrows go up, and his compliment to Ruby on her scores brings that blush back to her cheeks. It's not the only thing, either. Little baby wisps of fog are rising from her now like steam over a coffee cup. They drift through the air as if they're seeking a home, but nothing happens when they brush Kyle's skin. They just continue on.

I look away, picking up my glass again and focusing with everything I have on not absorbing a single trace of that mist. It'll only make this worse. But I don't want her to like him. On some deep, visceral level, I'm begging her to hate him, and I don't have a clue why.

Kyle crumples the wrapper of his food, and I jump at the sudden noise. Midway through setting my glass down, my hand flinches and almost spills the water.

"Whoa, sorry," he says. "Didn't mean to startle you."

"You sure you're okay, Cait?"

I nod. "Yeah. Just… thinking."

"Hope we weren't boring you," Kyle jokes.

"Of course not." My voice is entirely too sharp.

He simply smiles again. My muscles transform themselves into steel cables, almost ready to snap.

Turning the friendly expression on Ruby, he takes her tray and then stands. While he heads for the garbage bins, she never looks away from me. "Cait—"

I grab my backpack and rise to my feet, avoiding her eyes. She trails me toward the door, seeming torn between following me and waiting for Kyle.

He weaves past the tables quickly, catching up to us. "Late for class?"

I don't respond.

"I guess…" Ruby answers for me. I swear she's eyeing me like I've got two heads.

Kyle doesn't even seem to notice. "All right, well…" He grins once more. "We should do this again, yeah?" At Ruby's nod, he continues to her. "Care if I walk you to that International Policies class you were telling me about?"

"That'd be great. Thank you."

"My pleasure." He glances at me. "See you around, Cait."

I can't answer. I'm too busy searching for a reason for Ruby not to leave with him.

Nothing comes to me. They turn and start down the sidewalk, leaving me speechless and feeling like even more of a freak than I did before Kyle showed up.

What the hell was *that*? He's just a guy, for God's sake. A hot, nice guy who happens to have a lot in common with my best friend. That's a good thing.

Right?

They reach the corner and disappear from view. It takes me a moment to make myself turn toward the route back to my car.

Neurotic. That's what I am. Totally neurotic.

Hitching my backpack higher on my shoulders, I duck my chin to my chest and lock my gaze on the ground. I weave through the crowds, working hard not to bump into anyone. I don't want to absorb anything.

It's not easy. This is a campus. It's not as bad as the nightclub by any stretch of the imagination, but it's not exactly a nunnery. Every so often, I still feel mist licking at my skin, begging to be allowed inside.

My feet chew up the concrete, carrying me toward my car at a speed just shy of running. The quad falls behind me. The main roads too. I'm leaving the busier parts of campus, and my car is only another two blocks away. I risk taking my eyes from the sidewalk, and a breath of relief leaves me when I see only a scattering of people anywhere around.

I'll go back to my apartment. Possibly lock myself inside, but still. I'll be fine.

I wish Amar had given me his number. Not out of any romantic intentions—though, let's be honest, I wouldn't mind that either—but in case I needed help. But then, he'd been so cagey. Helpful, yes. He'd saved me back in the Physics Building. But there was still that weird reluctance, as if he wasn't willing to tell me everything.

Or to help me more than he'd already done.

My shoulders shift with discomfort at the turn of my thoughts. I'll just have to figure something out.

I tug my bag around and reach inside, searching for my keys while I round the corner to the road where I left my car.

Kyle's leaning against the wall of a building up ahead. His arms are crossed, and his ankles too, and he's got his eyes on the corner like he's been waiting for me.

I slam to a stop, staring. He can't be here. Not if he ran, not if he *flew*. I left him on the other side of campus, walking to class with Ruby.

"Hey, Cait."

There's something in his voice, his smile. Pleasant, but not like before. It's like we've dropped some game we were playing, and now the truth can come out.

"W-what are you doing here?" I sputter.

"Coming to see you, of course. We need to talk."

My brow twitches down. Rational Cait is yelling for me to run.

But suddenly, I'm not sure it'd do a damn bit of good.

"Talk?" I manage.

His smile becomes wry. He drops his gaze to the concrete like he's amused by me. "Cait, Cait, Cait. Did you really think we wouldn't notice? We damaged that Protected for a reason. We didn't want her simply put back together again."

My chest quivers. "I don't know what you're talking about."

"Really." His tone is dry. Contemptuous. When I don't respond, he scoffs. "All right, have it your way. We'll play stupid. I'm fine with that. So, *while* we're playing stupid, let me put it this way. I like Ruby. She seems like a lovely girl. Bit trusting maybe, but what human isn't? Especially once you start messing with them. And then keep messing with them. And then... well, it's not like there isn't room for another Touched in the pits, right? Especially if certain friends of theirs continue trying to be the hero."

His smile returns, cold this time. Cruel. I tremble at the sight, even as my head shakes. "I-I don't—"

Kyle laughs. "Sure you don't. We're playing stupid, remember?" He shrugs away from the wall, still grinning. "See you around, Cait. Tell House Linden I said hello."

He winks at me, and then turns and disappears around the corner of the building. I don't move to follow him. I suspect he won't be there anyway.

Just like Amar.

A gasp leaves me, harsh and breathy. He... what the hell is he? Not human. He can't be.

But he threatened Ruby.

Quivers radiated through my whole body, like I'm screaming inside. He threatened *Ruby*. I don't have a clue what he *meant*, but that doesn't matter.

I fumble out my cell phone and hit her number. It goes straight to voicemail. "Ruby? Call me, okay? Just call me the minute you get this."

I don't hang up, like it's some old-school answering machine and she can just pick up her phone to still respond to the call. But after a moment, the phone beeps and hangs up for me. I close my eyes, ordering myself to stay calm. She's in class. She wouldn't have her cell turned on anyway.

And she's fine. She's *got* to be fine.

I want to race back to her class right now to make sure.

Another breath leaves me. Actually, that's not a bad plan. It's on the other side of campus, but I can take my car and be there in a few minutes. I know what room she's in. It's just a lecture hall. I had a class there last semester.

Clutching my keys, I run for my car.

5

I'M LUCKY I DON'T GET PULLED OVER BEFORE I MAKE IT TO THE other side of campus. I think I left more than a few pedestrians on the verge of a heart attack in my wake.

My car skids into a parking space a block from Ruby's building. There wasn't anything closer. Not even a fire lane. I rip the keys from the ignition the second I come to a stop, and habit locks the door for me. I barely notice.

I tear down the sidewalk toward the massive stone building and veer wildly toward the door, yanking it wide the moment I reach it. The hallway is empty. Classes are still in session. My shoes echo from the marble walls, and I make myself slow when I reach the lecture hall door. The last thing I need is to burst in there like a deranged harridan and freak Ruby out.

Because she's fine. She's *totally fine*.

My grip trembles on the latch. I inch the heavy wooden door aside and peer through the opening.

Backs of heads. Tiered seats. Dimmed lights. A professor in a sports jacket and jeans, pointing to a chart on the screen at the front of the class. I scan the crowd, searching for Ruby.

And I spot her.

My hand clenches on the edge of the door. Her black ponytail is recognizable, as is the shirt she'd been wearing and the green jacket peeking past the back of her chair. She leans over, whispering something to the girl next to her, and the girl nods as if in answer to a question.

And nothing else happens. She's okay. Really, *actually* okay like I'd hoped she'd be.

I feel like crying.

Swallowing hard, I ease the door back into place, and for a moment, I just stand there, trying to calm down. Kyle threatened her. I know he did.

I just don't know what to do now.

On unsteady legs, I make my way back to the building's main entrance. Maybe I can warn her. I wouldn't really know what to say, since claiming that Kyle dropped her off and then immediately found me on the other side of campus is bound to sound insane.

Maybe I could just fudge a few of the details.

My stomach twists. I don't want to keep lying to her. Even the few lies I told today feel terrible.

It occurs to me that, given the *rest* of today's events and what I apparently am, I might not have much of a choice.

I bat the thoughts away. I don't want to think about that right now. But when it comes to everything else, when it comes to Ruby's *safety*, I have to do something.

I hesitate at the front door, one hand on the slick wood. I could just wait outside till she's done with class and talk to her the moment I see her. Explain that I didn't like Kyle. That he creeped me out. I could leave the inexplicable details out and stick to gut reactions.

Maybe she'll listen.

I let out a breath. That could work. Plus, class gets out in thirty minutes. Plenty of time to figure out exactly what to say.

I push the door open.

A man in a black suit is standing in my path.

Two sets of hands grab me from behind, one for each arm, and I look back fast. A pair of guys are there. Big guys. Like bouncer-huge. I feel something blunt and hard jab into my side, and I choke on a gasp.

"Don't scream," the black-suited man advises, like he'll be disappointed if I try.

My gaze rakes the area around us, but the few people I see are too far away to notice anything is wrong. "What is this?" I try, raising my voice in desperate hope that somebody will hear anyway. "I'm not—"

"Quiet," he orders.

A dark sedan with smoked windows pulls up to the curb as if summoned from thin air. The man glances to the guys holding me and jerks his head toward the car. They don't give me a choice. Gripping my arms, they force me toward the vehicle.

I open my mouth to yell.

The big guy on the left crushes his fingers down on my upper arm, grinding my muscles against bone, and my shout turns to a strangled cry. The other guy yanks open the door and shoves me toward the black leather interior. I can't scramble for the opposite side of the car. The driver turns the moment I'm inside, and I freeze at the sight of the gun in his grasp.

The man in the suit swings into the passenger seat while the other two guys take up positions on either side of me. I'm smashed in the center, trapped between two behemoths who could probably break my neck with one hand.

Ignoring them, the man motions to the driver, who puts the car into gear immediately. The sedan slips away from the curb like a shark, silent and smooth.

I look to the smoked windows, praying someone will point. Shout. Be calling the cops or filming the car on their cell.

But there's nothing. People walk by, glancing to the sedan perhaps, but not reacting like they noticed me being bundled in here like a rag doll.

The driver turns onto another road, and behind us, my car disappears from view. In the front passenger seat, the man pulls his phone from inside his suit, thumbs it on, and then lifts it to his ear. While he waits for the person on the other end, he glances back at me, and his icy expression doesn't change when they pick up.

"Got her."

PART II

6

THE CAR ROLLS DOWN THE ROAD WITH ME TRAPPED INSIDE. Two huge guys sit on either side of me like gorillas in suits, and no matter how I wrack my mind, I can't think of a way out of this. The windows are blackened. No one can see me. Shouting for help is pointless. The luxury sedan is sealed tightly enough to go into outer space. And everyone in the vehicle has a gun.

I can't imagine that'll go well.

Keeping my gaze on the behemoths around me, I inch my hand toward the cell tucked into my jacket pocket.

"Don't," the man on the left growls before my fingertips even brush the phone's plastic case.

I feel like screaming.

That won't help anything either.

"Where are you taking me?" I ask, working to muster up as much bravery in my voice as possible.

They don't respond. The sedan slides through the midday traffic like an eel.

"I haven't done anything. You can't just kidnap somebody off the street and—"

"Quiet," says the suit-clad man in the front passenger seat.

"I haven't *done* anything," I repeat. "I don't know what you—"

He draws his weapon from inside his suit jacket and points it at me over the seat, a look on his face like he's asking me if I want to continue.

I swallow hard. "You're not going to shoot me," I say, hoping desperately that the words are true.

He cocks the gun.

I tremble. His lip twitches.

The car slows and my gaze darts to the window. We're downtown now, miles beyond campus, and pulling up outside the entrance of some high-end restaurant. An awning stretches out over the entry and the sidewalk, its velvety fabric the color of blood, while a stoic-faced doorman waits by the entrance like a statue. The windows are mostly reflective, though a hint of shadows from within gives me the impression they also have their curtains drawn. The sedan cruises to a stop before the entrance, and immediately, the man in the passenger seat pushes open his door.

One of the men grabs my arm and starts from the vehicle. I scramble after him, gasping at the crushing pressure of his grip, and stagger onto the sidewalk.

The doorman doesn't even blink at the sight.

With my arm and the rest of me in tow, the behemoth strides toward the entrance, following the suit-clad man. The doorman moves with a robotic grace to open the closest of the glass double doors. I stare at him desperately, but he simply returns his attention to the street while the men haul me past.

Red velvet curtains flank the entrance, and a mahogany host station waits to one side. The molded tin ceiling is distant, at least thirty feet high, and the gold-trimmed lights are dim. The air smells like cologne—thick and cloying and vaguely spicy. My kidnappers continue onward, walking past a long bar on the right, the stools devoid of any customers and the bartender missing as well. A tall archway lies ahead. The lights are brighter in there. I can hear voices from beyond the arch, the words too low to be understood.

The men pull me with them into the room. People are there, but they're clearly not customers. Their hands folded in front of them in the manner of every bodyguard I've seen on television, they stand around the perimeter of the room. I can just guess that they have guns. Meanwhile, at a round, maroon-clothed dinner table in the center of the room, an old man sits. He wears a gray suit with a gray shirt beneath it, both of them only a shade darker than his silver hair. His pale skin shows no liver spots, no hint of blue veins, and his wrinkles seem almost artistically intentional. I'd swear he could be any age from sixty to a hundred. Turning his attention from the nearest bodyguard, he gives me a patient smile, as if I kept him waiting but he's decided it's okay. Other tables have been pushed aside ahead of him, leaving an empty space like a stage, while sunlight streams through the tall windows behind him, framing him in light like a human-sized god.

A door at the far end of the room opens. Suddenly, I can't decide whether to be surprised or horrified.

Amar walks in with two big guys behind him. They head for the old man, stopping a few yards away.

I gape at them, reeling. Amar set me up with… with *whatever* the hell this is? He—

My mind registers the tension on Amar's face. The way his dark, normally guarded gaze darts from the old man to me. He appears as expressionless as I've ever seen him, but there's an edge to it now, like he's fully expecting something to explode.

By contrast, the old man simply regards me with a vaguely amused look in his eyes. "Release her. I believe you've made our point."

The guy holding my arm hauls me into the empty space ahead of the old man's table and then drops his grip from me like an attack dog relinquishing a kill to its master. He doesn't even look my way while I rub my bicep, trying to restore the feeling to my arm.

"My apologies," the old man continues. "My people find it better to be safe than sorry."

"Safe from what?" My words are sharp. I can't help it, and my eyes keep twitching to Amar in a desperate attempt to read something about what's going on from his face.

I'd have better luck with a stone wall.

The old man's head cocks to the side as if my response intrigues him. "Well, *you*, mostly."

I stare at him.

"Tell me, my dear, what House are you with?"

My attention flies to Amar again. House? What the hell is—

Kyle had said House Linden before he walked away. Something about telling them he said hello.

I start to shake my head. "I'm not—"

"Why did you interfere with our Protected at the hospital?"

A breath leaves me. There's that word too. Protected. Amar said it. Kyle did as well, back on campus when he'd threatened Ruby.

"I don't know what you're—"

He turns toward the bodyguards behind him. "Take Mister Okoro into another room. I'll speak with him once we're finished here."

The men start toward Amar. He tenses, something predatory in his stance, but his eyes lock on me like I'm the one in danger.

My heart rate skyrockets. "Please, I don't know what you're talking about. That girl just grabbed me. I don't know what was wrong with her, but if I hurt her, I'm sorry. It wasn't intentional, I swear."

The old man holds up a hand, and his people freeze on their way to Amar. The man's eyes narrow at me. A moment creeps past in silence like it's afraid someone will notice it.

"Mister Okoro." The old man looks to Amar. "I was surprised to learn that you had involved yourself in such an affair. Is this why?"

Amar watches me as if he's weighing a thousand answers to a question I don't understand.

"*Is* she a Legacy, Mister Okoro?"

"She seems to be." Amar's voice is flat, giving nothing away.

A hint of a smile glides across the old man's face like an eel beneath the surface of a placid lake. "And is she unaffiliated as she claims?"

Amar hesitates again. "I don't know."

The old man makes a considering noise. "Has anyone tried to follow her?" he asks his people.

"No, sir. The House Volgert lackey appears to have only been sent to speak to her, nothing more."

"What did that young man say to you, my dear?" the old man asks me.

I blink. "You mean that—" I don't know how to describe Kyle. Creepy asshole? This doesn't feel like the place for words like that. "You mean Kyle? He threatened my friend. Said they damaged that Protected for a reason. Told me to tell House Linden he said hello." I shake my head. "I don't know what he—"

"No, of course you don't," the old man interrupts smoothly, and a bit distantly too, like he's thinking of something else while he says the words. "So tell me, my dear, why *did* you help our Protected?"

"Something felt like it was wrong with her. I didn't know what I was doing." I hesitate, my stomach sinking. "Is she okay?"

The eel smile comes back, humored this time. "Yes, she's fine."

I start breathing again.

The old man seems to catch the reaction. He eyes me up and down for a second and then glances at his people around the room. "I must say, I think we've gotten off to a poor start. You'll have to forgive us, dear. We were certain you were something else."

Nothing follows the words. No explanation at all. The old man just studies me like I'm some intriguing puzzle he happened to stumble across.

"Something like what?" I ask.

"When did you discover what you were?"

I glance at Amar. "Today. Though some of it started about a week ago."

The old man's brow twitches up. "Truly?" He pauses. "And your demonic parent, what do you know of them?"

I shiver. God, the words sound dreadful—and so does the fact he says them like he's describing the color of someone's hair. My brunette parent. My demonic parent. No difference at all.

My mind is rambling. It's better than focusing on the question, but then, he's still waiting for an answer. "Nothing," I say.

"So your feelings toward them?"

I flounder, uncertain how to respond. "Look, I don't know what you—"

"We were concerned you were an agent of a violent and dangerous House," he interjects like the conversational detour never happened. "Our world can be deadly for those without adequate protection. It even endangers my people, as you saw with our Protected last week. We—"

"What does that mean, 'Protected'?"

His lips press together ever so slightly, and Amar's gaze flicks toward him. I get the impression not many people interrupt the old man, no matter how he treats everyone else.

"My apologies," he says. "I jump ahead. Let's begin with introductions, shall we? I am Alistair Linden, patriarch of House Linden. And you are?"

I swallow hard. "Cait."

He waits for more and then smiles when it doesn't come. "It's a pleasure to meet you, Cait. A Protected is someone upon whom we've placed a bit of magic. A warning, if you will. One that alerts others like yourself to the fact that person is not to be fed upon, and which will severely harm anyone who tries."

I blink. Magic. Good God, he just said *magic*. And

worse, I think I know what he means. Those red threads. They'd surrounded her, fragmented and frayed inside the mist covering her body. The fog had been thick, as dense as any I'd seen at that nightclub, Temptation. When it touched me, it stung.

And that'd been *magic*.

On some level, I'm not shocked. I *should* be, but after nearly killing someone in a men's room, or after what happened at Temptation, or in the hospital, I've surpassed my capacity for surprise. I'm just carrying on like this is all normal now, like I'm riding it out in the hope that sooner or later it'll come to an end.

And maybe I'll wake up.

"Someone must have endured a significant amount of pain to hurt her as they did," he says.

"Hurt her how?" I ask, my voice choked.

His brow shrugs. "By driving her mad, and thus making an example of her to threaten us. Even as a Legacy —an individual born human and who inherited their parent's demonic abilities—you have the potential to be equal in power to any full-blood succubus. And that power has dangerous implications. You can do much more than feed on the sexual energy of others, Cait. If you choose, you can drive a human beyond reason, possibly never to return. Those humans become rabid creatures driven by lust and hunger, controllable only as wild animals—leashed and caged. They become the Touched."

I'm trembling, and not just because of the words. That's what Kyle's threat meant. That's what he hinted they'd do to Ruby.

Make her one of the Touched.

"This is the fate you saved our Protected from," he says. "For that, you have our gratitude."

My lips flinch into something resembling a smile, but I can't hide how it's strained.

"And, as a token of our gratitude, I have a proposition for you."

I freeze.

"What do you know of the Houses?"

I shake my head slowly. "Nothing."

The corner of his mouth rises, and it's easy to see I've confirmed something he suspected. There's something more there, though. I can't put my finger on it. I glance at Amar again.

He's still imitating a brick wall.

"Our world—and now *your* world—is ruled by Houses. Collective groups of individuals tied together by loyalty and commitment. Some of these Houses are vicious. Violent. They will stop at nothing to gain power, either over the other Houses or over individuals. Through our numbers, however, those of us with different goals have the strength to resist them. A House is a family, Cait, willing to do anything for one another. Willing to protect one another to the last."

He draws a breath. "And that is where our offer comes in. You are new to this world. You are alone, without a demonic parent to guide you or a House to protect you. Already, you've said one of your friends has been threatened. But we can help with that. Shield you. Give you the time and safety to discover what your new identity means, without the danger of someone preying upon you or those close to you." The old man pauses. "We do not make this offer lightly. Acceptance into a House is a sacred trust. But I can see you're a good person—a rarity among your kind. You helped that girl without thought for yourself even though she was a total stranger. House Linden would be honored to have you as the newest member of our family."

For a moment, I just stare at him. I don't have a clue what he's offering. He's spinning it like this is some simple choice, but I get the feeling it's a bit bigger than joining a sorority.

And there's still Amar.

I look at him again. He's on edge, possibly even more so than before. He's frozen, stone-like as a statue, and I can't even tell if he's breathing.

But he doesn't look eager. Happy. I've already figured out he's damn near impossible to read—two seconds at the hospital showed me that—but this…

"What does it mean?" I hear myself ask. "For me?"

"That you have protection," the old man says like it's obvious. "Friends to help you through this transition to a new life. From time to time, we may ask you to help us with small favors, but—"

"Like what?"

"Nothing you wouldn't do regardless. Sleep with people we send you to, in cases that require a certain degree of persuasion. You need to sustain yourself anyway, only now you can also benefit your House."

For the blink of an eye, I see Amar's mouth tighten like he's fighting back something. Like he feels sick.

I'm shivering. I don't know Amar, not really. I don't know any of them. But Amar helped me. There's something beneath that granite surface that's kind, even just a little bit.

Though now that I think of it—

"Why do you say I'm a rarity compared to… to others like me?" It's hard to get the words out, but I only stumble a little.

The old man pauses. "Succubi and incubi seldom care about anyone but themselves, Cait. And for a succubus to not only sacrifice her magic and energy for a *stranger*, but to give enough of herself to save one of the Touched?" He scoffs lightly. "Now that is an unusual creature, indeed."

"Then are you not a… you know?"

The old man smiles. "There are more things in this world than incubi and succubi, my dear."

It's difficult to fight back the shivers. They just want to grow stronger.

"So what is your answer?" he asks before I can pursue the question. "Will you do us the honor of becoming Cait of House Linden?"

I can't find a response. I don't want to be this. I don't want to be *here*. I feel like a child who's no sooner learned how to walk than they're being asked to run the New York Marathon. And that whole thing about sleeping with whomever they tell me to? My stomach turns at the thought of it. I don't know what I am anymore, but that sure as hell isn't something I want to agree to do.

And as for Amar…

My eyes linger on him. He's just standing there, not looking at me, not looking at anything. Is he with them? Amar of House Linden or whatever? Something inside me doesn't think so. Something that's reading his tension if nothing else, and the way that tension has done *anything* but go away.

I don't know him. But right now, I think I trust him more than anyone else in this room.

"Thank you," I say, trying to hold my voice steady and not show any hint of fear. There are still guns around me. God knows what might happen if I piss this old man off. "But… may I think about it? I'm not saying no. It's just…

it's been a hell of a day, and I only found out about this demon thing about an hour or so ago."

I swallow hard, not needing to fake the overwhelmed look on my face.

The old man pauses. The air panics and flees the room.

And then he nods. "Of course. This must have been incredibly trying for you." He glances at his people. "If you would please escort Cait and Mister Okoro back to their respective prior locations? I believe we're through."

The behemoths don't grab my arms this time. Instead, one of them turns, heading back the way we came while his buddy waits for me to follow. My eyes dart around and then catch on Amar. He glances toward me, hesitating for all of a heartbeat, and I can't gather a hint of what he's thinking from his face. Without a word, he walks toward a door on the far side of the room, not looking back.

A tiny breath escapes me, desperate. I don't know what to make of this, of his connection to what's just happened, of anything at all. I don't know when I'll see him again, or what to even *begin* to say when I do.

The behemoth at my side makes an angry noise, urging me to move. I can feel Alistair's eyes on me, still studying everything I do.

My skin crawling, I leave the restaurant.

7

ALISTAIR LINDEN'S PEOPLE DEPOSIT ME BY MY CAR, SPEED OFF, and in only a second, it looks like the last hour never happened. Sure, a few vehicles have moved from their parking spaces. Classes have changed. But the afternoon has gone on like it's any other day.

I'm beginning to feel like a tennis ball, slapped back and forth between what seems normal and what is unequivocally insane.

I stand beside my car for a few moments, fidgeting with my keys while I debate trying to find Ruby in her next class. I've missed the end of the last, that much I know, but I'm not sure I remember the correct room number for the current one. We compared schedules at the beginning of the semester, but all I recall is it's some combination of one, two, and five.

Frowning in frustration, I climb into my car. I'll wait for her at the apartment.

And she'll get home just fine.

I exhale, struggling to push down my fear. I need to

come up with a way to keep her safe from Kyle. Maybe through figuring out how to make her one of those "Protected," or maybe something else entirely. But I will.

And without joining up with some House I know nothing about.

My stomach twists. This is madness. My whole life has become madness in the space of a single week. One single week that feels like it's lasted for an *eternity*.

The drive home passes in a blur, and I find a spot down the road from my building on autopilot. Hefting my bag over my shoulder, I hurry along the sidewalk toward the enormous, brown-sided house that the landlord converted into a tangle of cheap apartments.

Amar is waiting inside.

I slam to a halt. On the linoleum-covered steps that lead toward the upstairs apartments, he's seated with his elbows braced on his knees and his hands folded like he's been waiting for a while. He regards me, his dark eyes unfathomable.

"What?" I sputter. "How did you—"

"I followed you and your friend when you left the hospital the other day. Saw where you lived."

My brow climbs. Oh-*kay*, that's a bit stalker-y. More than a bit. What the hell?

He seems to see something of my thoughts in my eyes. He turns away, an expression on his face like he's kicking himself. "It's just... things in our world, they're—"

"Dangerous, I know." I bite off the words. I've had about all I can take of this. I don't know whether to scream or cry after the day I've had, and he's...

Hell, he's the only target I've got. It's not a good reason, but right now, I almost don't care.

I let out a breath, ready to snap at him again, but he simply glances up at me, unfazed.

"Yeah."

My fury falters at the quiet agreement in his tone. At the look in his eyes, like he knows *so* much more about this than anyone has said thus far.

And for a moment, I want to race past him. Climb the stairs as fast as I can and disappear into my apartment. Maybe lock the door. Maybe hope that'll work to keep all this out. And just hide.

Amar sighs. "You should come with me."

"Why?"

"Because you need help, and I have a friend who might be able to provide it."

He rises to his feet. I stare as he walks past me.

"Why should I trust you?"

He pauses but doesn't turn. "I can't answer that for you. Whether you trust me is up to you."

That's not a good answer.

Hell, there *is* no good answer. What should he have said? Because we're cosmically destined to be together, thanks to Quantum Physics class and sheer luck?

What would I believe anyway?

He looks over his shoulder at me, solemn, like all the world could quake around him and he wouldn't be moved. "You'll be safe with me, Cait. I promise."

Without another word, he pushes open the door and steps out into the sunshine.

My mouth moves, and I don't have a clue what I want to say. But I believe him. I don't know why. I couldn't begin to explain it if I tried.

But I do.

My eyes twitch toward the stairs and my apartment on

the third floor. I could still run, though. Maybe I even should run.

But I need to protect Ruby.

And no matter how much I want to, I can't make myself believe this is all just going to go away.

⸮⸮

We walk to my car, and from the moment he sees it, Amar seems concerned.

"You drive this?" he asks.

I bristle. It may not be much, but the boxy little Toyota is mine. A sky-blue piece of crap with rust spots and a rattling muffler, maybe. But still mine.

"You can take your own," I suggest.

He hesitates. "I didn't bring it."

I stare at him, a question in my mind I can't quite bring myself to ask. One that touches on everything from his presence before I got hit by a car to Kyle suddenly being on the other side of campus from where I left him. "How did you get here?" I try instead.

Amar's gaze skims over the neighborhood. Old houses surround us, most of them converted into apartments, and towering trees line the road. Across the street, a guy is walking a dog while a few students are hanging out on a porch several houses away from us.

"We should leave," he says rather than respond. He takes the handle, and I see him hesitate again, like he's weighing whether the car trip will be his last.

"Look, if you want to catch the bus instead or something—"

"It's fine." He opens the door and then pauses for a second when he sees the books I've got sitting on the seat.

A couple of indie fantasy authors I requested the local library order a few weeks back. His eyebrow twitches up, and I can't quite figure out how to read the sudden amusement in his eyes, but he doesn't comment as he climbs into the passenger seat and carefully sets the books aside.

I get in and try not to wince when the door hinge squawks like a startled goose.

Amar fastens his seatbelt and doesn't say a word.

"Where to?" I ask tightly, not looking at him.

"Head downtown."

I put the car into gear and then pull from the parking space. The old houses fall behind us quickly and fancier places follow: upscale apartments and fashionable brick office buildings, interspersed with monolithic churches that probably predate everything in a five-mile radius.

My eyes dart to the churches and then away. I've never been much for church. Went a couple of times with a friend from elementary school, but it never really stuck.

Now I'm just glad I didn't burst into flames when I walked through the door.

The old trees of the area give way, and downtown appears ahead of us, all towering steel and glistening glass. Corvinson doesn't have skyscrapers. Not yet, anyway. From the way Arlene's friends in the Chamber of Commerce talk, though, I get the impression the local officials like to pretend these twenty- and thirty-story buildings are coming close.

Long shadows fall around us when we drive between the towers. The low rumble of the muffler drowns the rush of traffic.

Amar glances at me. "Take the next left."

I flick the signal and then guide the car where he directed.

"Parking garage with the blue sign on the right. She has spots reserved inside."

My eyebrows rise when I realize where we're going. What building this garage belongs to. Chastain Plaza. The fanciest—and tallest—of the non-skyscrapers in town.

I pull the car inside and park in the spot he points out, and then I turn to him. "Your friend is here?"

"Her father owns the building."

I blink.

Amar pushes open the door. "Come on."

A heartbeat passes before I can follow him. Milford Chastain is one of the richest men in… well, this town, for certain. But probably in many circles beyond Corvinson too.

And we're going to meet his daughter. His daughter who might be a demon.

I wonder what that would make him.

Swallowing hard, I hurry after Amar, my footsteps echoing off the concrete ceiling and floor. At a set of steel doors on the far side of the garage, he stops. He doesn't glance at me when he presses the button to call the elevator. His gaze is on the wall and distant, like he's thinking of something else.

The doors part and roll back. We walk inside a box of gleaming brass and polished wood, and he pushe the button for the top floor. A moment passes in which nothing happens, and then he looks up at the tiny security camera on the wall like he's waiting for someone.

The doors shut. The elevator car rises through the building. Amar drops his gaze back to the wall, thoughtful again.

I watch him from the corner of my eye. It's more than thoughtful. He's back to closed-book mode, although it's not like it was at the restaurant. Now he's calm. He looks like a bomb could go off and he wouldn't flinch.

The elevator car slows. The doors open. My eyes widen.

White walls. Marble tiles on the floor. Paintings in colors so rich, they seem to absorb the light. Glass tables line the spaces between the enormous pictures, their surfaces glistening beneath the sparkling chandeliers hanging from the ridiculously high ceiling. Double doors wait ahead of us, their dark wooden surface gleaming with liquid-like varnish and their golden handles catching the light.

Amar leaves the elevator and strides toward the entrance. I follow, my eyes darting around and finding more cameras. Motion sensors. Little things I can't even identify, clinging to the ceiling and almost certainly monitoring us in some way. I tug my attention back fast when he opens the doors.

My expression doesn't change. The place looks straight out of a lifestyles article on the rich and famous. White carpet sprawls out in front of us, down a short flight of steps, and then across a spacious room dotted with elegantly understated furniture. More art hangs from the walls while vases and sculptures of glass sit below them. A grand piano stands before windows that reach from the floor to the distant ceiling and stretch for the entire length of the far side of the room. A pair of dogs are resting on lamb wool cushions by the base of the windows, Dobermans both of them, and their heads lift when we come inside.

I tense, but the dogs don't move.

Footsteps sound on the staircase that runs up the right

wall. I tear my gaze from the dogs to see someone with candy-pink high heels descending toward us.

"Amar?" a young woman calls. "I thought you had class."

"You did too," he points out, a touch of dryness to his tone.

Light laughter follows. "Yeah, well. I didn't feel like being *bored* today."

The young woman comes into view. She's about my age, taller than me by several inches, with thick golden hair that curves in artful waves down her back, and she's wearing a simple dress that probably cost more than my car. The pink fabric clings to her sides and hips and then flows out till it reaches her knees. She swings around the end of the staircase, her pale hand balancing her on the banister, and her rose-colored lips curve at the sight of me.

"Oh," she comments idly. "Who's this?"

"Cait, Bianca Chastain. Bianca, Caitlin Faire." He pauses. "Cait's a Legacy. Just found out."

Bianca seems to look me over anew, amusement taking up residence in her blue eyes. "Really? How in the world did you miss *that* for so long?"

She says it like I must have been in a coma to have accomplished something so ridiculous.

"I didn't *miss* anything." It's difficult to keep the bite from my voice. "This only just started."

And I have *no* idea why.

I leave the last part out. I'm growing more uncomfortable by the second, and suddenly, I don't want to admit any more ignorance to this girl than absolutely necessary.

Her face takes on a quizzical cast, like I'm some weird little creature who just showed up in her living room. I turn to Amar, unsure what I'm supposed to make of this. I came here for help, not to be treated like a freak because I didn't know I was a *demon*.

This is the friend who's supposed to help me?

"Bianca," he says in a tone like he's telling her to play nice.

"What? It's a fair question. She's a decade beyond when most of you find out."

Amar just looks at her. She makes an exasperated noise, rolling her eyes as if seeing something in his complete lack of expression. "God, fine." She turns to me. "*Sorry*. Now, what's going on?"

"Linden Protected," Amar says. "Last week."

"And?"

"Cait saved her." Amar nods toward me. "So Alistair Linden had us both brought in for a chat."

Bianca shrugs like she couldn't care less. "Well, if you're here, I'm assuming it went okay, so what's the problem?"

"They invited Cait to join House Linden."

"Do you want to?" She looks at me.

I blink. "I don't know them. Amar just told me about this demon thing today."

She scoffs, and I honestly can't tell if the noise is meant for Amar, the situation, or just me and how I "missed this" for so long.

Amar ignores the sound. "She needs another option," he says to Bianca.

At this, Bianca freezes. Just for a millisecond, but it's there. And then she laughs. "Oh my *God*, Amar, I'm not getting tangled up in this!"

"Bianca—"

"No. No way. You've seen what's going on. Volgert's acting like they want to tear Linden apart, and Linden's given every sign of being ready to return the favor. The minor Houses are staying out of it, but you *know* Ivanov, Hartsfeld, and Akbari are just waiting to see who draws first blood before jumping in too. God knows why they've all decided to lay into each other *this* time, but seriously. Why the hell would you think I'd stick my neck anywhere *near* that?"

"New York."

The pause comes again, longer this time. "That was different."

"Make it not be."

"This isn't *like* that, Amar."

There's an edge to her voice, sharp and hard.

"Linden wants to add Cait to their collection," he counters evenly. "And from what she's said, Volgert's after her too. Her demonic parent is gone. How is it different?"

Bianca shifts her shoulders like she's shrugging off his words, and she retreats a few steps away. "Listen, if she wants to come feed at Temptation, that's her business. Everyone's welcome there—as long as they follow the ground rules, anyway. I don't care. But that's all I can offer."

"She needs to know about the rest of it."

"So *you* teach her!" She throws up her hands like she's done with us. "God, what is this, *charity hour*? You want to adopt some Legacy without a clue, be my guest. But don't go dragging me into it."

My blood starts to boil. Amar doesn't respond.

For a heartbeat, Bianca stares at him, an expression spreading across her face like he's just grown horns. Her gaze flicks from him to me. "Wait, what is this? You're not—"

"No," he interrupts like the unfinished question disgusts him. "Of course not."

Her gaze rakes over him like she's evaluating whether she trusts the response. Amar's jaw muscles jump with repressed anger, as if she's insulted him, though I can't figure out how.

"Um, listen," I say into the awkward silence, keeping my voice as level as I can. "I don't know what you guys have going on here, but I just need someone to do that Protected thing, okay? I don't want to get involved in any of this."

Amar gives Bianca a look like my words just proved something for him. She doesn't reply but pulls her attention from him to me instead. "What's so important about the Protected?"

"Somebody threatened my friend. Said they'd turn her into one of the Touched. That Alistair guy said the… that *thing* protects people from being hurt. I want someone to do that for her. Keep her safe."

Bianca scoffs. "Do you have *any* idea how much energy it takes to put magic like that on some human? And… what? I'm guessing this friend doesn't even know about us? Considering you apparently just found out and all?"

"No, she doesn't."

She rolls her eyes again. "Oh God, and she'll be unsuspecting too. I'm sorry, but that's—"

"I can do it," Amar interjects quietly.

Bianca gapes at him. "Are you out of your *mind*? Magic like that will knock even *you* out of commission for days and leave you starving besides, and with the Houses at each other's throats…" Her gaze goes between us again like she's watching something repulsive play out before her eyes.

Amar turns away. "The more they start snapping up Legacies at the moment of their inheritance, the less content they'll be to leave the rest of us alone."

"They're not after *neutrals*, Amar. They don't care—"

"Right. Until they start a war." He turns back, meeting her gaze flatly. "You think they'll just come for me if that happens?"

Bianca looks away.

Amar nods as if the motion proves him right. "We don't need some girl running off and giving the Houses ideas just because of a temporary situation, Bianca. This is the only hook Linden has managed to get into her. So let's just fix it."

My stomach twists at the ice in his voice. At his words: "some girl." The term stings.

For a moment, Bianca doesn't move. "Fine," she snaps. "You want to do this… fine. When?"

She directs the last to me. I struggle to regroup. "Um, help Ruby, you mean?"

"Yes."

I fidget with discomfort, not quite looking at Amar. "Soon as possible, I guess. I don't know what that guy plans, so—"

"And we're doing this wherever the girl lives, I'm assuming? Considering she's unaware of us and all."

"Probably best," Amar replies.

"After she's asleep, though," Bianca insists. "Unless, of course, you *want* her to know about you?"

She raises an eyebrow at me, and I don't know what to say. Want Ruby to know I'm apparently this whatever-the-hell-I-am? Oh, yeah, sure. That'd be an *awesome* conversation.

Though it might make things easier when it comes to

Kyle. And it'd be nice to have someone to talk to who wasn't deep into this. To whom I wasn't a stranger or "some girl."

I push the thoughts aside. "I can let you into the apartment tonight," I say rather than answer the question.

"Good enough." Still appearing irritated, Bianca spins and stalks back toward the stairs like she's done with us.

Then it's just Amar and me in the cavernous space. And he's not looking at me.

"Thank you," I say. "For, you know, agreeing to help Ruby."

He doesn't respond while he heads for the door.

My stomach sinks. Right. Friends, we are not.

Some girl.

Exhaling briefly, I shove the pain down and trail him out of the room.

"We'll come by around midnight," he tells me when we reach the elevator. "Will she be asleep?"

I nod. "I think so."

Amar echoes the motion. His eyes twitch toward me, and for just a moment, I think I see something uncomfortable in his gaze. But then it's gone, swallowed up by that stone-faced look that seems to be his default.

He pushes the button for the elevator. The doors roll open immediately.

"See you then," he says.

I hesitate. "You're not coming downstairs?"

"I need to clear something up with Bianca."

I glance back toward the open door of the apartment. The girl is nowhere to be seen. There's a hardness to Amar's words, too, as if that flash of anger I saw from him earlier hasn't quite faded.

I nod again. It's not like there's anything else to do. "Okay, well, see you tonight."

"Yeah."

I fight back any sign of a reaction to the terse response and flee into the elevator. My fingers hit the button for the parking garage quickly, but I can't stop my eyes from twitching to him when the elevator doors start to close.

He's watching me. "Tonight," he says, his tone softer, almost like an apology.

And then the doors shut and my view of him is gone.

8

I'M PACING MY BEDROOM BY THE TIME THE CLOCK HITS midnight, and every little sound from outside makes me jump. Ruby went to bed an hour ago, exhausted after an evening shift at the restaurant where she works as a waitress. I retreated to my bedroom not long after, if only to avoid questions if she happened to come back out into the living room. It's left me trapped in here, though, with only a few feet of space between my bed and the window. I'm starting to feel like a caged animal. I only hope Ruby is sound asleep.

And that I'm not making a mistake by trusting Bianca and Amar.

I take a deep breath and keep pacing. I don't have much of a choice. Yes, Bianca seems like kind of a bitch, but she and Amar are my best option. And yes, Ruby would want me to talk to her about this first, but I can't have that conversation. Besides, if this goes well, Ruby won't need to know anything has even happened. Hell, no one will.

I spin through another turn. That's the crux of the matter, really. The past few hours have clarified some things. Now that I don't have muscle-bound behemoths with guns around me or, even worse, Kyle anywhere nearby, things have started to crystallize. I don't *have* to be a part of this. I really don't. I can walk away.

So I will. I'll be done with these demons and their world, Ruby will be safe, and I'll never have to tell anyone anything about this crazy week at all. Who cares if I'm not like other people? If I'm not *human*? I already spend most of my time feeling like I don't fit in; how's this going to be any different? I'll just move on, figure out how to handle whatever I am, and I'll do it without becoming what Arlene always swore I'd be. A slut like my mom. A whore who tears apart families. It's ignorant, puritanical bullshit, I know.

It burns all the same.

So it's fine. This'll be over soon. I'll never have to see Bianca, Alistair, Kyle, or anyone else from this past week ever again.

Including Amar.

My stomach twists. I can't help that. I wish I could, but I can't. Sure, he's hot. Intelligent and sexy all in one gorgeous, intriguing package. I'd love to get to know him better. I'd love to break through that granite exterior to learn more about the guy I catch glimpses of underneath. It's only been a few days, I know, but over and over, my thoughts turn to him with countless impossible little fantasies that can't ever really be. Because I can't be part of this world. I can't stay to figure out what—if anything—he feels for me or whether those flashes of… of *something* I see past all his stoicism are really the interest in me that I hope it could be.

But if they are…

A stifled noise of irritation escapes me, aimed entirely at myself. Who am I kidding? What about today, huh? He made it clear to Bianca he only sees me as an inconvenience, and he's only helping me and Ruby out of enlightened self-interest or whatever. And you know what? So am I. Kyle is a threat. Amar and Bianca provide my best chance of keeping Ruby safe. End of story.

My hands wring against each other. It's really… really just the end of that story.

A quiet knock comes on the front door.

I lurch to a stop, my thoughts pulling up short. I throw a startled glance to the street, but I don't see any cars I don't recognize.

The knock comes again.

Abandoning my confusion, I bolt out of my bedroom. The living room is a tangle of shadowy furniture and textbooks, picked out by the faint glow slipping past the curtained windows. In my haste, I stub my toes on the coffee table, and a choked cry escapes me.

My eyes dart to Ruby's door. It stays closed.

Sucking air through my teeth, I stagger across the remainder of the room. Hobbling a bit to keep the weight off my foot, I tug open the door.

Amar and Bianca are standing there. He's wearing his dark jacket just like earlier today, and she's dressed in a knee-length cream coat above a pair of glossy, eggshell-colored flats. They look like a shadow and a ghost in the dim hall.

Concern tinges his expression at the sight of me. "You okay?" he asks in a low voice.

"Yeah. Just…" I feel like an idiot. "Nothing. Come in."

Bianca breezes past me. Amar follows more slowly, his

eyes lingering on me like he's not sure he trusts my answer.

His attention makes my heart race, and I look away fast, searching for anything to distract myself. "I didn't see your car outside," I whisper.

"We didn't drive," Bianca replies.

I blink.

She looks to Amar and her mouth tightens. "I'll explain later," she promises, more to him than me.

Amar doesn't respond, and I'm not sure what to do. Still casting uncertain glances at them both, I head for Ruby's room, weaving a wide path around the damn coffee table. At her door, I pause, listening intently for any sound she's awake.

Silence. I take the handle and inch the door open.

Pale light from her window spreads over the bed, picking out her form beneath a blue comforter. The slowly pulsing light of her sleeping laptop and the green glow of the alarm clock are the only other sources of illumination in the room. Watching her for a moment, I wait to see if she'll wake up. When nothing happens, I glance back at Amar and motion for him to follow.

I slip past the door. Books, binders, and papers form teetering stacks on every available surface, and their shapes are nothing but odd shadows against the darkness. Snapshots of the two of us, of family, and high school friends hang from a string along the left wall. I feel like their eyes track me while I sneak across the room.

Ruby shifts in her sleep. I freeze. A second creeps past, and then I look behind me. Amar is there, and Bianca is beyond him, leaning on the doorframe with her arms crossed. Her mouth is a thin line, but I'd swear she seems almost more concerned than annoyed.

Soundlessly, Amar steps past me, his eyes on Ruby. At the side of her bed, he pauses and then extends a hand toward her sleeping form. He draws a deep breath and lets it out slowly.

Blue light spreads from his palm, ghostly like fog. White flecks dance inside it, and as it brightens and lands on Ruby, the light changes. Turning to glimmering blue tendrils, it brushes across her face.

Ruby's brow furrows. Her lips rise in a small smile, though, and she gives a contented murmur. Mist begins to rise from her skin.

My face blazes scarlet and I look away fast, realizing what's happening. What she's probably dreaming about now. And it makes sense, given what Amar is. I probably should have expected this. But it still makes me want to leave the room and possibly erase the past few seconds from my mind. I'm already way past invading her privacy. I'm standing over my best friend in her own bedroom, letting a near-stranger do some sort of bizarre magic on her in the hope of keeping her safe. But watching her reaction to what's probably some kind of erotic dream *so* feels like the last straw.

My gaze catches on Bianca. Her eyebrow twitches higher at me, like she doesn't get what the problem is.

Uncomfortable, I pull my attention back to Amar.

His eyes are closed. There's a tightness to his face, like he's struggling with something. His hand is shaking. My gaze snaps to Ruby, to the fog around her. Glistening sapphire threads run through it now. They're twisting around her, weaving a complicated path amid the fog. But it's nothing like what I saw from the girl in the hospital. There are millions of them, encasing her like a cocoon, without a fragment or frayed edge to be seen. I can't tell where the threads begin or end.

Amar drops his hand away from her. The glowing blue mist fades. After a heartbeat, the fog around Ruby sinks back into her skin and takes the sapphire threads with it.

He shakes his head like he's trying to clear it, and then he glances back at Bianca. She rolls off of the doorframe and leaves the room. Amar starts after her.

I follow, watching Ruby while I leave. Her breathing is slow and steady. She seems to be sleeping even deeper than before.

"You didn't have to do *that* much," Bianca hisses at Amar. "Good *God*."

He doesn't answer.

Gently, I ease the door closed. "You all right?" I whisper to him.

"Fine."

He's not looking at me. His head is hanging down, and his shoulders rise and fall like he's working to keep breathing. Bianca's watching him too. It's obvious she doesn't believe his response in the slightest.

"Okay," I try. "But do you need to sit down or—"

"We should go," Bianca interrupts flatly.

Amar nods. He grimaces as he straightens, though the expression fades when he glances at me. "She might seem more tired than normal in the morning. She'll be fine, though."

"Thank you." I mean the words more than I can convey.

For just a moment, there's something in his eyes, and I can't quite read it. Understanding, maybe. Sympathy.

It's gone as fast as it appears. "Yeah."

He heads for the door.

Bianca begins to follow him and then pauses at the entryway, looking back at me. "Come by my penthouse tomorrow. We can get started then."

"Get started with what?"

"Teaching you what we can do."

What? No. That isn't my plan. My plan is to be done with this. To handle it on my own.

Though it might help to know what else I'm up against in "handling" this, just in case.

I bash the traitorous curiosity down fast. I don't need Bianca's help with that. I need to stay out of this. Besides, what Amar did in there was amazing, sure. It's great that he could help Ruby. But the rest of what we can do seems to involve sex, and while it doesn't matter to me if someone is a lesbian or bisexual, I'm not really into that myself.

Unless she means…

My face flushes. I can't stop my eyes from darting in Amar's direction. I am *so* not doing this. "Um—"

Bianca makes an exasperated sound. "Go," she snaps to Amar. "Brett's expecting you at the club."

Amar hesitates, his eyes twitching to me, but after a moment, he nods.

He turns and starts down the hall.

And then he's gone.

I stare. Not "turned the corner" gone. Not "it's so dark I can't see him" gone.

Literally *gone*. Between one step and the next, just at the edge of where the window at the end of the hall has cast a square of light on the dim corridor, he's simply disappeared.

Bianca looks back at me. "See you tomorrow."

And then she vanishes as well.

9

I TAKE THE NEXT DAY OFF WORK. OFF CLASS. OFF EVERYTHING.
The library where I hold a job as a shelver will survive just
fine without me, and right now, my classes can go to hell
for all I care.

In the parking garage outside Bianca's building, I sit in
my car and try to breathe. Ruby was tired this morning,
just like Amar said, but otherwise, she seemed fine like
he'd promised. She even had a hint of a grin like she'd
slept better than usual, something that left me distinctly
uncomfortable. I did my best to ignore it and pretend this
is just a normal day, for her sake as much as my own, but
that didn't stop me from fleeing the apartment at the first
opportunity.

Even if it only ended me up here.

I look toward the elevator at the far end of the garage. I
shouldn't be here. Not really. I called in sick to work and
avoided everything else out of sheer desperation, but that
doesn't mean I should take Bianca up on her offer. Her

order. Her whatever-that'd-been. I can handle this on my own. I can survive without anyone's help. I'm good at that.

But then, the two of them had disappeared into thin air.

Who knows what else they can do?

Shivers course through me. Their kind could show up anywhere. Could *find* me anywhere. What if I can learn some kind of defense against that?

I grab the door handle. I'll just learn about the disappearing thing. Then I'm done.

My phone rings.

I jump a mile before I recognize the sound, and a litany of cursing runs through my head while I scramble for it. I really should change the ring tone. It keeps freaking me out.

Or maybe it's the circumstances.

I snag the phone from my bag, swipe my thumb across it to connect the call, and then my eyes register the number.

The cursing in my head gets more vehement.

"Caitlin?" Arlene snaps before I can even say hello.

My hand tightens on the door handle. "Yes?"

"You need to come over to the house. Now."

The floor drops out on my stomach. Dad. Oh God. "What's wrong?"

"Your father insists on seeing you."

"Is he okay?"

"Are you going to take long? Because I really cannot—"

I hang up and toss the phone into the passenger seat while I yank my legs back into the car and then slam the door. The engine grinds when I crank the key too long in the ignition.

He has to be all right. He *will* be all right. He's fine.

The car flies backward when my foot crushes the gas pedal. I haul the gearshift around and then floor it. The muffler roars, echoing from the walls of the parking garage.

But nothing goes fast enough. The traffic. The stoplights. If ever there was a time I wish I knew that damn demonic disappear-into-thin-air thing, it's now.

The house looks completely normal when I arrive. Well, almost normal. Kelly's and Bethany's cars occupy the driveway. But ambulances and police are conspicuously absent.

I screech to a halt near the curb and flee the car. The gate bangs back against the picket fence when I rush past it, and my shoes thud hard on the steps to the covered porch. I snag the brass handle and shove past the front door.

Kelly and Bethany turn. They're seated on the couch, their auburn hair in glistening waves and their postures ramrod straight like Barbie dolls. Their blue eyes widen at the sight of me.

"My God, Cait," Bethany protests. "Where's the fire?"

I stare at the twins for a moment, gasping. "Where's Dad? Arlene called and—"

"Oh, for pity's sake," Kelly interrupts. "He's just upstairs."

I shove the door closed behind me and take off up the steps. I hear Kelly make a disgusted noise behind me, though Bethany doesn't say a word.

But then, she's always been the nicer of those two nightmares anyway.

I swing fast around the banister at the top of the staircase. Dad's room is down the hall.

I can hear his voice inside.

A ragged breath enters my lungs. Outside his door, I stop. Closing my eyes briefly, I try to slow my racing heart. I can't make out the words—he's just murmuring—but he still sounds okay. Not gasping. Not dying. Better than he's sounded in a while, actually, even if he's speaking softly.

I swallow hard and then push the door aside.

"But, John, I just don't think it's appropriate that you stress yourself. She can—" Arlene cuts off at the sight of me.

I don't spare her a glance. "Dad?" I cross to his bedside quickly and drop to my knees beside him.

The weathered lines around his blue eyes crinkle when he smiles. "Caitie."

I bite my lip briefly. He's the only one who calls me that. The only one who's allowed. "Hey." I reach out, taking his hand where it lies on the emerald-green comforter. His thin fingers close around mine, and hope bubbles up in me at how his grip is stronger than it's been in ages. "How're you feeling?"

"He needs his rest." Arlene bites off the words. I don't turn. She doesn't exist right now. I'm not letting her take this from me.

"Has the doctor been here yet?" I persist.

"Caitlin—"

"It's all right," Dad breathes. "Could you give us a second?" His brow rises at Arlene, gently questioning.

I can feel the ice coming off of my stepmother in waves. "Of course, darling," she replies, enough sweetness in her voice to send an elephant into sugar shock.

Her footsteps pad away. The door closes. I don't let myself believe she's not listening outside.

"Your mom has a tendency to worry, Caitie," Dad says. "You know that."

I nod for his sake.

"So tell me how school's going," he says. "Anything new happen lately?"

Tears try to rise, and I choke them back. "I want to know how you are."

He smiles. "I'm fine. Doctor's coming soon. But I was a bit tired last time you were here, so right now, I want to catch up on my girl's life."

My fingers tighten on his, carefully, gently. I nod again. "It's, um…" My mind runs through the insanity of the past few days, and then I shove it all aside. "You remember how I told you about my math professor? The one with the uneven sideburns and the paper bits stuck in his hair?"

Dad smiles. "I remember."

I grin. "Yeah."

And for a little while, life is better than normal.

THE DOCTOR ARRIVES LATER, BUT BY THEN, I'VE HAD A COUPLE of hours with Dad—longer than I've had in years. I know Arlene is seething over it, but I don't care. For the first time in ages, I have a shred of hope that my father might get well.

Arlene is waiting for me outside the door.

I push past her and toss a smile to the doctor who's here to see Dad. If I'm lucky, Arlene will be caught up enough in taking care of the doctor that I can make it out the door before she comes after me.

I barely reach the base of the stairs.

"You selfish little brat. What were you thinking,

stressing him like that? Taking hours of his time all for yourself?"

I keep moving.

Arlene snags my arm, yanking me around. "You listen when I'm speaking to you."

I tug away from her. "He wanted to see me. You said so yourself."

She scoffs.

I start for the door again.

Arlene storms across the living room after me. "I don't want you dropping in without my permission anymore, you understand me?"

"I'm his daughter. I'll visit him if I want."

"No, what you *are* is a burden to him, Caitlin. You always have been. One needy, selfish, spoiled little burden. And now you're not around. You think it's a *coincidence* that he's suddenly getting better?"

I spin back to stare at her. Behind her, I can see Kelly smirking like she's enjoying the show while Bethany is studiously engrossed in a cookbook she found lying on the kitchen counter.

And I'm shaking. Trembling so hard it hurts, and all I want to do is scream at her. I know it won't go well. That it *will* stress Dad out and only prove her right. But I want to hurt her for the accusation. I want to cut into her the way she always tries to cut into me.

Rage crackles through my veins. The hairs on my arms stand on end.

"Mrs. Faire? May I speak with you?"

The doctor's voice carries down from the second floor.

"Of course," Arlene replies pleasantly.

She starts up the stairs, only to pause and look back at me. "You're not welcome here, Caitlin. Leave."

I shiver. My eyes track her as she walks away.

"What is it, Cait?" Kelly asks sweetly. "Got a hearing problem?"

My attention snaps over to her. "Shut up, bitch."

I storm from the house.

1 0

I DRIVE AIMLESSLY. I LOSE TRACK OF TIME, ENDING UP AT GOA Cafe.

And I'm still so furious I don't know whether to punch something or cry.

I purchase a latte and manage to sustain some semblance of small talk for the time it takes the cafe owner, Pradeep, to make the drink. He's a short man, barely my height, and old enough that he probably should have already retired, but he runs the cafe like a machine. Chatting with customers is a requirement for him, and normally, I'm up for the conversation. But today, just his smile when I take the drink almost proves too much. Ducking my head, I pretend I didn't see the expression and retreat to the upper level of the restaurant. The tables in the back corners are all taken, though. Without any other option, I find a spot by the wooden railing overlooking the first floor.

Time creeps by. The doors open and close. The lunch hour gets underway... passes... dwindles off into the afternoon. My latte remains in its white mug on the table, untouched.

Arlene had no right to speak to me like that. Neither did Kelly.

Funny how that never stops them.

My nails dig into my palm. Kelly's been like that my whole life. Arlene's little lackey. She's the older of the twins by all of sixteen minutes, and she's always seemed to resent the fact that I got here first. Like being the eldest is anything worth fighting over. She loves how Arlene treats me, though. Seems to view it as proving she should have been the oldest one.

And Bethany…

My mouth tightens. Silent accomplice. Turtle who never leaves her shell. She's just happy she's not the one they pick on, and if push comes to shove, she's instantly on their side, like the kid who holds the bully's stuff so he can kick some other kid's ass.

Though neither of them compares to Arlene.

My nails bite deeper into my palm. Today wasn't anything special. She's said that kind of crap before, blaming me for Dad's illness. I shouldn't have let it bother me. It's not like she has anything to base it on, besides her own vindictive bull—

Unless she knows about me.

The thought brings all others to a halt.

Could Arlene know? But how? She's not been involved in my life in the slightest, at least not where anything besides berating me for existing is concerned. She *couldn't*—

But what if she did?

Ice creeps through my veins. What if it *is* me? What if the whole reason Dad's been sick my whole life…

My stomach churns. Oh God, what if Arlene is right?

I stare at my latte, unseeing. It's not possible. What we do is sexual, and for me to hurt Dad… That's sick. I may have issues, but they're damn well not *that* kind. It *couldn't* have been me that hurt him.

My biological mother, though…

I want to cry. It's not *possible*. She's been gone for years. My whole life. Dad didn't start getting sick till I was four. Amar said that if we stop feeding and the person gets better, they'll be fine. Dad was fine for nearly half a *decade*. There's no way anything my birth mother did would have suddenly kicked in at that point.

At least, I don't think so.

I shove the thought away. It's not me. It's not anything to do with me.

But then why does Arlene always say I'm the one to blame?

I reach for the latte, only to stop when I realize it's long since gone cold. Grimacing, I set the mug down and turn back to the view of the first floor.

Four guys are walking into the restaurant.

I recognize them.

The ice inside me gets worse. The memories are fuzzy —the day they come from was hell—but I know who the people down there are. The friends of that guy I nearly killed in a men's room.

I shove away from the table, and my chair scrapes on the tile floor. One of the guys looks up at the sound. I gasp, retreating fast.

He didn't see me. He wouldn't have seen me. The shadows on the second level are thicker than on the first floor.

I have to get out of here.

My eyes sweep the area behind me and then lock on the exit sign glowing in the far corner. I bolt toward it. The stairway behind leads to the cafe's back door. Frantic, I race down the steps. The steel door slams against the brick wall when I burst past it, and I wince as much for Pradeep as the fact those guys could probably hear it while I tear down the alley.

I'm freaking out over nothing, though. I'm edgy because of this damn day. They won't come after me. I'm being absurd.

The four guys run around the corner. "Told you I saw that bitch!" one shouts.

I skid to a stop with a desperate cry. My hand fumbles for the pepper spray in my bag, though my eyes never leave the guys.

They fan out, blocking the alleyway. "What the hell did you do to him, huh? He spent two days in a damn *hospital* because of you!"

The four of them start toward me.

"Please." I retreat. "I'm sorry. I didn't mean to hurt anyone. Please, I just—"

The nearest one grabs my wrist. "We're taking you to the cops, bitch. You're going to pay for what you did to him."

He twists my arm behind my back. Pain shoots through me.

And that's not all.

A sensation envelops me, like the air is instantly sucked from the world into me. And as quickly as it happens, it reverses.

The guy rips away from me and flies toward the brick wall of the cafe. His friends stumble back and crash to the ground.

"What the—" one of them cries.

I stagger, my legs suddenly struggling to hold me. My muscles feel shaky. Electrocuted.

The guys clamber to their feet, not taking their eyes from me. One of them grabs their friend and helps him up. "What the fuck *are* you, you freaky—"

"Hey!" Pradeep rushes from the café's rear door. "What's going on here? You leave her alone!"

The guys look from him to me, and then they retreat and run like hell once they reach the sidewalk.

"Are you okay?" Pradeep asks me.

My head moves in some autopilot version of a nod.

"I'm calling the police," he growls.

"No!"

He pauses at my shout. I gasp for air. I can't stop shaking.

"Cait, are you *sure* you're okay?" Pradeep starts toward me.

I stumble away from him, my hands raised to keep him back.

He stops, a baffled expression on his wrinkled face.

"I-I'm fine. Just… no cops. I'm fine."

"Those boys tried to hurt you. I saw how upset you were in there; were they the reason for that? Did they follow you? Are they threatening you?"

"Pradeep, I'm *fine*." I work to make my voice sound calm. "It's nothing."

I don't wait for more questions. Turning quickly, I flee the alley as fast as my legs can carry me.

It's dark by the time I feel calm enough to handle going back to the apartment. I don't want to give anyone a reason to ask me questions, least of all Ruby. I want to pretend like this is just a regular day. I want to hang onto normal, or at least try to find it again.

And forget I blasted four guys away from me with whatever the hell that'd been.

My hands start shaking.

In a parking space on the street outside my building, I close my eyes and clench my fingers on the steering wheel. I can handle this. I'll just go upstairs, tell Ruby I'm not hungry, *hope* she lets that excuse fly for a second time this week, and get into my room as fast as I can.

No problem.

Exhaling sharply, I release the steering wheel and push open the door.

Amar is waiting on the steps of my building.

I freeze. For a moment, it's all I can do not to scream.

"Cait." He pushes to his feet and starts toward me.

I retreat fast. "What the hell are you doing here? Are you *stalking* me?"

He pauses. "You never showed at Bianca's today."

I don't know what to say. I feel ragged and frayed like the threads in that hospital girl's Protection. "I never said I was coming."

"You need help in this, Cait."

"No, what I *need* is to be left alone! I need everyone to just leave me the *hell* alone! What the fuck is it to you how I handle this, huh? You just can't keep out of other people's business?"

Amar doesn't move for a moment. His jaw muscles jump. "Fine."

He turns to go.

My feet move before I register the impulse. "Wait, no. Amar, I'm sorry. Please."

He stops. I shiver hard and hug my arms to myself. I can't take this out on him. I don't even know why I am, except maybe it's because he's safer than anything else in this crazy, apparently demonic world. But, God help me, that's not a good reason. That's not any kind of reason. That's just cruel.

And I can't drive away the only person with answers.

I wet my lips, trying to calm down. Answers, he might have, but right now, I sort of don't want them. I don't think I'll be able to handle any more revelations, any more information about how much of a freak I've become. I just want it all to stop. I'm going to shatter if this madness doesn't stop.

But I want him here too.

"Thank you," I make myself continue. "Thank you for checking on me. I just—"

He glances back. My stomach flip-flops for no good reason.

"I'm sorry." I choke out the words again.

He looks up and down the street quickly, almost like he's checking for something, and then he comes back toward me. "What is it? What happened?"

It's hard to breathe. "Bad day."

He pauses. His attention flicks around the neighborhood again.

And then his hand takes mine.

My breathing stops. His palm is hard. Strong. Warm, but not like he's nervous. His dark eyes don't leave mine, and I can't tell what I'm seeing in them. They're just so deep, I could drown.

"Come with me," he says quietly.

He turns, and my feet hurry to follow. My mind is stalled in that moment, though, reeling from the instant his fingers first touched mine.

We cross the grass, come to the corner of the house. The streetlight illuminates the yard, but the glow ends in a sharp line of shadow when it reaches the wall's edge.

Amar looks back to me. "Deep breath. Don't let go of my hand. Concentrate on staying with me."

My brow furrows. His rises in response.

I nod quickly. I draw in a lungful of air.

He steps forward into the shadow, bringing me with him.

The air goes cold. Sharply frigid like a blast from a freezer for all of an instant, and then it becomes cool. Mist-like. Darkness blurs in front of my eyes like rushing fog on a moonless night. And then it's over.

I stagger onto a grassy slope. We're on a hill at the edge

of a dark forest, and a swath of silver-touched grass is spread out ahead of us beneath the bright moon. In the distance, lights glisten. The city. We're miles from town.

"You all right?" Amar asks.

I tug my focus to him. "What—" I swallow hard. "What was that?"

"Shadow-crossing. It's one of the ways we get around."

My head moves in a nod, as if those words were anything approaching normal. His mouth tightens.

"Over here." He doesn't let go of my hand when he starts toward the tree line.

I follow. A park bench comes into view amid the shadows, tucked away beneath a massive oak tree. I can see the dull line of a sidewalk behind it, the concrete weaving a serpentine path through the woods, and I realize we must be in Glacy Park, the nature preserve outside town.

He sits down on the bench, and I join him, but then his hand leaves mine. I battle back a surge of disappointment.

"So what happened today?" he asks me.

I tuck my hands away inside my sleeves and bundle my arms tightly against my stomach. I don't know where to begin, so I don't. "It's nothing."

He's silent.

The words come anyway, grudgingly. "Some guys today. Friends of that boy that I... It's not important."

"Did they hurt you?"

I can hear an edge in his voice, cold and sharp as a knife. I shiver. "No."

He doesn't speak.

"It's not just them," I admit after a second. "It's this day and..."

"What?"

"It's stupid."

"Why?"

His voice is so quiet. So gentle that it makes my eyes burn for no damn reason. I look away, fighting the tears.

"My stepmother hates me. How classic, right?"

He doesn't say anything.

"My dad's sick. Doctors don't know why. Been like that most of my life, but today, he started to do better." I hesitate. "He wanted to see me."

Silence follows. I swallow hard.

"Arlene just… she said a lot of shit. It doesn't matter."

"I'm sorry."

I look over at him, and it's there. Sympathy. Clear as the star-filled sky above me and nothing like how he disguises his feelings so thoroughly most of the time.

"Do you have family?" I hear myself ask. "Near here or…"

His face shuts down. He turns his eyes to the field like he's closing the door on me.

My cheeks flush scarlet. I drop my gaze to my lap. Bad question. Never mind. Shit.

Seconds creep past. Somewhere in the distance, night birds make quiet sounds in the darkness.

"A sister."

I blink at the words said so softly I can barely hear them. I look back at him.

He's still watching the field. "Mother and stepfather too, I think."

"You think?"

Amar hesitates. "I haven't seen them since I was sixteen."

My eyebrows rise.

"My father came for me when I was twelve," he continues. "Showed up one day and said it was time to go. I'd never seen him before, only knew he was my parent because of my mom's and stepdad's reactions." His lip twitches. "She started screaming at him. Grabbed a kitchen knife to drive him out of the house while my stepdad went to call the cops." The smile fades. "And my father slammed them both into the wall without even touching them. Said he'd kill them if I didn't leave with him."

I hug my arms tighter to my middle.

"So I did. Things had already started to go strange for me: seeing fog around people, getting this weird rush when it'd touch my skin. I thought maybe I could do something to him, hurt him somehow so he couldn't keep me or threaten my family again."

He shakes his head, futility clear in the motion.

"My father was a very powerful incubus. Cruel. Cold. He was based out of New York, and he worked for Volgert. And over the next four years with him, I saw things, *did* things…" He takes a deep breath. "But I also met Bianca. Her family. I think I was a curiosity to her. The scrawny little Legacy kid who never said a word. But when my father died, she gave me a place to go. A way to avoid getting sucked into the Houses and falling even deeper into their mess."

"But you didn't go home?" I ask.

He shakes his head again.

"Why?"

Amar glances at me. "Because I'd seen our world."

A shiver runs through me at the look in his eyes.

He returns his attention to the field. "I put a Protection on them all, and I never came near them again."

I watch him for a moment. He keeps doing that. Talking about the demons in this way like he's haunted.

But to leave your family… to never see them again because of your own choice, because you were just trying to keep them safe from the horrors you'd witnessed… I don't know if I could do it. *Choose* to never go near Dad again. Know that he was out there somewhere, and just hope that he was okay.

It makes me wonder what Amar's seen in the years since his asshole father yanked him away from his home.

I reach out and wrap my fingers around his. "I'm sorry."

Amar doesn't move. He doesn't even seem to breathe. For the longest moment, he just sits there, his gaze locked on the field and his hand frozen in mine.

And then, ever so gently, his thumb slides along my hand, back and forth, back and forth, like he's testing the feel of my skin.

My breath catches.

He pulls his hand away and rises, all in one swift motion, as if the tiny sound of my breath snapped him out of the moment we were in. "I should get you home."

I stare up at him. He's gone cold in that weird way he has, all ice over a surface of rock. "O-okay…" I push to my feet. "I'm sorry. I didn't mean to upset you."

The ice cracks, just a bit, and regret shows through. Regret and determination, anyway. "Please," he presses, a touch less harshly. "Let me just take you home."

My brow flickers down, but I nod. He turns and heads toward the forest.

I trail after him. At the edge of the shadow of the trees, he reaches back without looking at me.

Eyeing him, I take his hand.

Amar steps forward. Darkness rushes around us again.

He drops my hand like it burns him the moment we're

back in my yard. "Bianca's out tonight, but she'll be around by tomorrow evening. Come over then. She can teach you about shadow-crossing and whatever else you need to know."

He's gone before I can even respond.

1 2

THE DOORS ROLL BACK, AND IT'S DIFFICULT TO LEAVE THE elevator. I've been cursing myself the whole way here, swearing I can handle this on my own and don't need anyone's help—though I'm starting to wonder how much longer I can convince myself that plan stands a chance in hell.

And I want to see Amar.

I step out before the doors can close, and I take a breath in the cool, dry air of the hallway. There's nothing saying he'll be here. Nothing saying he'll be anything but cold after whatever happened last night. But I still want to see him. I want answers for what the hell went wrong.

And the truth is, I probably do need help.

My legs tremble. It just keeps getting worse, that shakiness. I thought maybe it was simply a muscle cramp from sleeping wrong, but all day long, it hasn't gone away.

I'm afraid of what it might be.

Stilling my face into the closest semblance of calm I can muster, I cross the hall and willfully ignore the cameras tucked in the corners of the ceiling. Bianca knows I'm here, I'm sure. She's probably known since I got in the elevator.

Taking another deep breath, I pull one of the double doors aside. The apartment looks the same as before, all white carpet and expensive art. The massive wall of windows on the far side of the space lets in the last rays of light from the fading sunset outside, and the distant ceiling makes the whole room feel cavernous. I don't see Bianca, leading me to think she's still upstairs, but when I reach the steps to the main area, I catch sight of someone else who makes my feet pause.

Amar is seated by the windows, over near the corner with the Dobermans, which rest at his side. He's looking out across the city, not giving any sign he knows I'm here.

I swallow hard and continue into the room. "Hello?"

"Cait," Bianca calls down from the second floor. She appears by the stairway and gives me a polite smile.

Amar doesn't turn around. He might as well be a statue.

I force a smile onto my face and return my attention to her. "Hey."

"*You* stood us up yesterday," she says brightly, coming down toward me.

"Uh, yeah, sorry about that."

The smile comes back. It reminds me of painted plastic. "No worries. I think we got off on a bad foot, anyway. So…" She starts into the living room. I follow. "Amar wants me to teach you magic. Help you get a handle on what we are and what we can do. I think he believes it'll be easier, you and I both being succubi and all."

She casts a barbed glance at him. I realize the speech is for his benefit as much as mine.

Amar doesn't turn around.

"I figured we'd begin with something simple," Bianca continues to me, the barbed look vanishing. "Summoning up some magic. Getting a feel for that, since shadow-crossing is a tad advanced. That's what we call that thing you saw the night before last, by the way. How he and I left your apartment building. We can hold off on that for the moment. We'll get to it, though. No sense leaving a succubus out there who doesn't have a clue what she can do, right? You'll probably just end up screwing things up for the rest of us."

I hesitate at the words. "Um, okay."

She turns away again. My attention flicks to Amar. He hasn't told her about last night.

And he still isn't looking at us.

"All right," Bianca begins. "So, I want you to hold out your hand."

I stretch my hand out in front of me, feeling a bit ridiculous.

"There. Yeah. Just like that. Concentrate on your hand. On feeling the blood in your fingers. The air on your skin. Now, I want you to picture a light—"

I gasp as a purple fizzle of electricity crackles to life in my palm. It sputters and snaps and then dwindles into nothing like a dying flame.

"Well," Bianca says. "That's not *much*, but it answered you faster than I suspected it—"

My legs buckle like all the energy has suddenly fled my body. Bianca moves quickly, catching me before I drop to my knees.

"Holy shit, girl," she protests.

I push away from her, regaining my feet. My lungs are working overtime to draw in air, but after a moment, the weakness in my muscles fades.

Bianca stares at me. "You're drained."

I gulp down a breath.

"Cait, you're drained," she repeats. "How the hell are you this drained? Amar told me you fed only a day or so ago."

I don't know what to say. Or how to have this conversation, especially with her. "I-I think I used up what I had."

"How?"

I hesitate. "Some guys."

Amar turns his head ever so slightly, like he's actually listening.

"Guys?" Bianca presses.

"Friends of the guy I, uh… the guy from a few days ago. They attacked me in an alley. Grabbed me, and then…"

"You got rid of them," Bianca fills in when I trail off, amusement in her voice.

"They just flew back. I don't know how, but…"

Her brow rises. "Flew back? Damn." She sounds impressed. "And from a blast strong enough to use up all your energy… you didn't kill any of them, did you?" She seems far more humored than concerned.

I falter. "No."

Bianca chuckles. "Well, this isn't going to work. You need energy to do what I was planning today—*any* energy. You're going to have to get out there and feed on somebody, girl."

I feel a blush starting to burn its way up my neck.

"What?" Bianca protests when she sees me hesitate. "Hit the club. Brett will take care of you."

"Brett?"

"Yeah."

My gaze darts around. I remember them mentioning him the other day. Brett waiting for Amar. Brett at some club. "Who, uh… who's Brett? Your boyfriend?"

Bianca bursts out laughing like I just said the funniest thing she's ever heard. *"What?* Oh my *God,* no. Brett's my brother. He owns Temptation." She scoffs at me, a look creeping onto her face like I'm a moron. "Boyfriend. God, Cait, what do you think we are, *human?"*

I stare at her, confused.

She laughs again. "Oh dammit, Amar. You didn't say anything about that, did you?"

He doesn't turn. "It wasn't important."

"Yeah, to *us.* Cait here still thinks like one of them." Bianca looks back at me. "We don't date, girl. We don't do *love.*" She says it like a dirty word. "Not like that. Romance is for humans who think their hormones can't be swayed with a simple touch, and who let their emotions drag them around by the nether regions all day long."

Still laughing, she shakes her head and then catches sight of my expression. I don't know what's on my face, but when she sees it, pity joins the amusement in her eyes. "Oh, Cait, come on. It's training, you wanting that. Just humans trying to make you like them. Are you telling me you've ever actually felt a *single* thing for the guys you let into your pants? *Really?"*

I don't respond. I can't.

"Yeah, didn't think so. You're a demon, girl. Half human too, and it'll try to mess with your head if you let it, but that's not the point. Deep down, you've always been a demon, even if that side didn't wake up till now. So you don't have to be bogged down like they are. All that shit just makes them vulnerable. The faster you let go of that human side of you, the happier you'll be."

I blink, dragging my gaze from her to Amar and back. Oh my God, this is it, isn't it? The reason he never lets anything out.

The reason he probably never will.

I feel like I can't breathe.

"Look," Bianca says. "Just go to the club. Find some hot piece of ass and have a good time. No regrets. No need to carry on like it's going to be anything more. Just a great, fun fuck, and you'll feel all better in the morning."

I want to be sick. My head starts shaking of its own accord.

Bianca's brow furrows like she's baffled by my reaction, and then suddenly, the confusion changes. "Wait. No. Oh my *God.*"

Amar's head turns toward us at the sound of her surprise.

Bianca gapes at me. "You're… you're a virgin, aren't you?"

My traitorous skin flushes scarlet.

"How the *hell* did you manage not to—" Her jaw drops, and she turns away, pressing a hand to her mouth like she's trying to contain a laugh.

I glance at Amar. He's back to watching the city like he couldn't care less about our conversation.

Bianca motions like she's trying to calm her own amusement down. "Okay, not a big deal. I mean, unless you're, like, uber-religious or…" She seems to be reading my reactions. "No. All right, good. But you're *definitely* going to have to get that virgin thing taken care of. Damn."

My eyebrows creep up. What?

"You're inexperienced," she explains. "First time you get some guy inside you, you're going to lose control. It wouldn't be such a big issue if you were younger. You wouldn't be strong enough to cause too much damage. But now?" She makes a knowing sound. "You'll kill the poor bastard. You have to get a grip on this if you're going to avoid becoming a murderer, all right?"

It's difficult to even blink.

"Look, it's not a problem." Bianca turns. "Amar, you busy tonight?"

I want to melt through the floor. Evaporate. Run like I'm being chased by the hounds of hell.

Because I sort of feel like I am.

Amar doesn't even turn around. "I can take care of it, yeah."

My mouth falls open. *Excuse me*? He literally just agreed to sleep with me with the same degree of enthusiasm he'd give to picking me up for work in the morning.

Bianca looks back to me. "See. Easy." She spots my expression. "Oh, come on. Amar's *super* experienced. You'll have fun."

I don't think. I just start for the door.

Bianca catches up to me in a heartbeat. She grabs my arm and pulls me around. "Cait."

I jerk at her grip. It doesn't budge.

"Cait." Her humor is gone. Insistence is all that remains. "Listen. You *will* kill someone, all right? If you don't do this properly, some poor schmuck out there is going to *die*. We all go through it, the rush of that first time. But you *have* to learn to control yourself, or you'll end up a killer, you get me?"

Her blue eyes are fixed on mine. I can't breathe at the look in them. Cold. Determined. Knowing. It's horrible. Like she can just picture me murdering someone. Like there isn't even a question.

The guy in the men's room flashes through my mind.

The expression on his face when he fell. Two days in a hospital, his friends had said.

My mouth moves, soundless. My head manages a nod.

She releases my arm. "Go to the club. Both of you. It's Friday night; tons of people will be there. It'll be fun. Get you enough energy to at least practice *some* magic here. And then just have a good time taking care of that other detail. Come back tomorrow, and we'll start working on everything."

Amar pushes to his feet. Mine feel like they're rooted to the floor. He walks past, sparing Bianca a quick nod and not looking at me at all.

"Go," Bianca orders, shoving me lightly.

It breaks my paralysis. Numb, I follow Amar to the elevator. I arrive just as the doors open, and I trail him inside. The doors roll shut.

He doesn't look at me. "It'll be fine."

I stare at him. Fine. Sleeping with me tonight will be *fine*, he says. Fine like… like what?

I wonder how many girls he's been with. When he just "got it over with." He's *experienced,* Bianca said.

And speaking of Bianca…

"Have you slept with her too? Bianca?"

The words blurt out of me, tense and almost hysterical with incredulity. But he just pushes the button for the garage, and when he speaks, his tone is as empty of emotion as I've ever heard it. "Yeah."

I sort of want to die.

13

We don't take my car.

In the leather-upholstered bubble of Amar's Audi, I keep my gaze to the window. I don't ask how he affords it, this black knife of a vehicle. I don't say a word. I stare out at the passing city and watch the lights go by.

I thought I'd seen beneath something with Amar. I thought there was more to him. Something deeper than the ice he shows everyone else.

But now I'm not so sure.

Now I'm wondering: who knows him better? Me? Not likely. Or Bianca, the girl around whom he's spent the past decade?

Not important, he said. The fact their kind—*his* kind, *Bianca's* kind—viewed love as a joke wasn't important. Meanwhile, Bianca didn't give his reaction a second thought. She just laughed like his statement was a foregone conclusion.

From the way he's been treating me tonight, I'm suddenly wondering if I should have seen it as one too.

Sleeping around. Bit obvious that would be the case, given what they are. Treating sex no differently than ordering a drink at a bar. Also probably something I should have expected. He doesn't have feelings for me. He's one of them—mind, body, and soul. There's no way he could.

Which means I'm just some task he's attending to tonight.

My fingers ball into fists. I want a way out of this. Some way to fix the situation. I get that I'll end up having sex eventually. Hell, I'd have thought I would've had it sooner than this too. It wasn't intentional, this whole virgin thing. It wasn't like I was saving myself or something. I just... it never came up.

It never had a chance.

A shiver runs through me. I dated two guys in high school, if you could call it dating. The first was a miscalculation on my part—I hadn't realized his dad was in Arlene's Rotary Club. She found out about it. Lied to his father. Next thing I knew, the boy wouldn't speak to me. Nasty rumors—*horrible* rumors—started circulating about me. It wasn't until I befriended Ruby and she told her popular friends the stories were bullshit that I stood a chance of overcoming that.

And the other hadn't listened. Came to pick me up at my house because he'd been certain it would be romantic.

He ended up dating Kelly.

But being a virgin isn't only because of my disastrous attempts at relationships. I live on my own. I'm getting my degree and probably going to grad school after that if I can figure out how to fund it. The last thing I need is an accidental pregnancy or some goddamn STD.

So my nonexistent sex life isn't intentional. It's just happened that way.

I didn't picture it changing like this.

"You want me to come inside the apartment with you?"

I blink at the sound of Amar's voice. We're parked outside my building. I'm not sure how long I've been sitting here, staring at nothing. "Whatever."

I push open the door and leave the car. A moment passes before I hear him follow.

The cool air clears my head a bit. I start walking faster, putting distance between us as quickly as I can. I don't want to be near him. Don't even want to look at him. Not anymore.

I bolt up the stairs.

Ruby's in the living room. She looks up in surprise when I barrel past the door. "Hey, what's up?"

I gulp down a breath. "Nothing. Listen, are you going to be around tonight?"

"What? Oh, um, no. Probably not. I have this thing with my activist group. We're staging a sit-in to protest the homophobic bullshit that place downtown pulled last—"

"Okay."

Her brow furrows at my quick interruption.

Amar saves me from an explanation. Knocking briefly, he leans around the open door. "Cait?"

Ruby's brow climbs. "Hi."

I look away fast. "My room's there." I gesture vaguely. "Can you give me a minute?"

He pauses and then heads inside without another word. The door shuts.

Ruby rounds on me instantly. "Is that your *date* tonight?" she hisses, her eyes wide. "Oh my God, Cait. I knew you had it in you, but *whoa*, is he hot."

I don't respond. I know he is. Good grief, I know he is.

I feel sick.

"Cait?" Ruby's excited expression is gone. Alarm has taken its place. "You okay?"

I swallow hard. "Yeah, sure."

She lowers her voice, her gaze darting toward the closed door. "What is it? What's wrong?"

I can hear the beginnings of full-blown protective mode in her voice, and I shake my head fast. "Nothing."

Her caution doesn't fade. I flash some cracked version of a smile and hurry after Amar.

I find him on the opposite side of my room, regarding a framed picture of Ruby and me. He glances over, and his brow twitches up, questioning, when I come inside.

I snag the emerald dress I borrowed from Ruby the other night out of my closet and make a beeline for the bathroom, closing the door behind me. My heart racing, I lean against the wood.

This sucks.

Tears blur my gaze and I squeeze my eyes shut. I'm being ridiculous. I never expected true love the first time I had sex. Not really. Maybe. Possibly not, anyway. But that's still a *far* cry from this. Some guy fucking me because I need to get it over with.

It's like he's helping me get the tires changed on my car.

My fingers ball into fists and press to my midsection, trying to stop my stomach from roiling. Bianca said someone could die if I didn't do this. Someone *would* die. And she's probably right. She's almost certainly right.

The rational part of my mind stares at me, arching an eyebrow. Really? She was right in saying I should sleep with Amar—this sexy, intelligent, *incredible* guy to whom I apparently mean nothing? And then what do I do? Pretend I felt nothing too?

Yeah. Right.

I hug my arms closer and sink to the ground. I'm edgy, and it's no mystery why. I've nearly used up whatever the hell I took in from that guy at school. And I know Bianca's not wrong, claiming that I'll need more soon. Desperation is gnawing at the edges of my mind already.

So I need to get out there. Go to the club. Do what Bianca said.

My body is shaking. My eyes burn.

I'm still just being ridiculous. Big deal, right? Who cares? Sooner I lose my human side, the better off I'll be.

My fist digs deeper into my middle, and my lips crush down on each other, stifling any chance I'll make a sound Amar will hear. He's right outside, after all. He's probably wondering what the hell is taking me so long.

Nothing is. Well, nothing beyond the fact I can't do this, anyway. "Getting it over with" be damned, I won't be okay sleeping with him and then carrying on like I couldn't care less. I can't be like them. Like Amar. I'm too drawn to him. Too attracted and intrigued by those damn dark eyes and that closed-book mask and that shred of humanity I wanted to believe he had somewhere inside. I can already imagine how much pretending I don't care that he doesn't give a shit about me will hurt.

I don't want to do that to myself.

I won't.

Resolution settles over me like a slow fall of snow. I really won't. I *can't*. He's too… too *something* to me.

But maybe some stranger won't be.

I shift against the door. I know what Bianca said. How hard it would be to control. But I'm not new at this.

Not completely. Sure, maybe I lost it with that one guy, but then again, he *didn't* die. And I've inadvertently ended up feeding off quite a number of people by now, thank you very much, if you include the dance floor the other night. So maybe I *can* control it. I didn't know what it was before, but now I do. So this is different. No, it's not romantic. It's not even all that appealing, sleeping with some stranger like this. But it's going to happen eventually, and how much better to just kill two birds with one stone—take in the energy I need and get losing my virginity over with, right? That's what Bianca was arguing. So maybe this is better. Clearly, the whole sex thing isn't about *love* or even affection to demons anyway. Might as well burn that ideal to the ground now.

But I don't need to tell Amar. He probably won't care—for him, this whole virginity thing is just some minor check mark on a to-do list—but it's still not his business. I'll let him take me to the club, grab the first non-repulsive guy I see, and finish this.

Simple. Easy. Whatever.

I push back to my feet, and it doesn't matter how hard my body is shaking. How weirdly cold I feel. It's been a long week. I snag the dress from the ground and set to getting changed.

⁓

My sandals slap the concrete, and music pulses through the walls of the club. The dark night air is colder than a week ago, and it makes the hairs on my arms stand on end. We walk to the door, and I see several people's brows rise when we bypass the line entirely and continue inside at a wave from the bouncer. The man simply nods to Amar, though, who nods back.

I wonder if the bouncer's a demon too.

We pass through the dark hallway and out into the bar. We're not touching, per Amar's suggestion. It's easier to attract people if they think we're just friends.

Gazes linger on me. Him too. Fog drifts around us, caressing me, slipping into my skin, taking the edge off.

Amar glances at me. "Drink?"

My attention flicks to the bar, considering, but I need every scrap of control I can get if I want my plan to succeed.

I shake my head.

He continues toward the gallery overlooking the dance floor. My body rigid with tension, I follow.

Rainbows of light spin in the darkened room. In his booth above the mob, the DJ is focused on his music, barely sparing a glance to the dancers below. The floor is packed, though. The music pounds around us, darker and more sensuous than the first time I came here. And I can see right away that it's having an effect. The mist hanging over the crowd is so much stronger than before.

My lips part. I can practically taste it in the air.

Amar touches my arm. I flinch, my control faltering for a moment. I scramble internally to hang on to my resolve. I don't care what he thinks. What Bianca said. I'm going to make this work.

I'm not somebody's damn chore.

I pull my arm away. "What?"

He hesitates for only the barest fraction of a heartbeat, but I see it. The question in his eyes, the curiosity at my sharp tone. He nods to the stairs, his eyes still on me.

I turn my focus to the dance floor and scan the shifting

crowd for a target. It's hard to spot anyone in particular from up here.

Better to just get down there.

I stride past him and head for the stairs. I don't know if he follows. I don't care. Bodies crush around me when I reach the lower level, and fog does too. I take a sharp breath, forcing myself to let it in. To relax. Because I can do this. No problem at all.

I slip deeper into the crowd. Hands grab me. People push against me. I lose sight of Amar almost immediately, but that doesn't matter. My hands reach out, brushing against the strangers all around.

It feels good. So good. Someone's up against me now, hands on my hips, body pressed to my back, and I grin. I glance over my shoulder, and the guy matches my smile with a whole lot more lust mixed in. He's a dark-haired guy, maybe twenty-five, wearing a t-shirt with the cartoonish logo of some band.

He'll do.

I twist in his grasp. Touch his cheek with my fingers and see something in his eyes change. They go hazy like the guy at school, even if I didn't realize it at the time. I'm doing something to him.

Drug, Amar said. What we can do, it's like a drug.

I nod to the far side of the room. The guy's grin widens. I take his hand. He follows me out of the crowd. Up the stairs. Into the restrooms. I want privacy. Apparently, so does he.

He's on me the moment the stall door closes. My back hits the side wall, and then his mouth hits mine. His hands grab at my hair, my shoulders, while he drives his tongue against my own, hungrily, greedily. Energy pours into me, thrilling through my veins, making me smile against his lips.

But it's still not enough. Two birds, one stone. I can do this.

I let go of his back, fumble lower, find the closure of his jeans. He hesitates only a moment, but he doesn't need another invitation. His hands are under my skirt instantly, sliding up my thighs, bunching the green fabric around my hips. His palms are hot, sweaty, and his fingers clutch at me for a moment before catching on my panties and tugging the thin fabric down.

Lust is pouring off him like a torrent. I lean my head back, trying to breathe, trying to pace myself. I have to be careful. Have to stay in control.

His fingers slide between my legs, slipping against my clit, sending a jolt of pleasure up through my brain.

That's all it takes.

I choke on a gasp, and my eyes go wide. The torrent hits me a hundred times stronger than before, and I don't stand a chance in hell of stopping it. I feel like my mind is exploding with ecstasy. Like I've taken every drug known to God or man. My visions blurs. Blood rushes in my ears, drowning everything. My nails dig into him, hanging on as he falters and his weight sags against me, and I'm killing him. I *know* I'm killing him, but this feels so good that I can't move to make it stop—

The stall door rips open. Amar is standing there, absolute fury on his face. He snags the guy, tears him away from me, and sends him to his knees outside the stall. And I can't help it. I start toward him.

Amar grabs me, slams me against the wall, and then his lips are on mine.

Pure energy pours into me. It's hot. Blinding. My world

vanishes in a blast of white light while heat surges through me, shredding my thoughts, my lust, and leaving only a stillness like the universe has chosen this moment to stand still.

Amar pulls away from me. His gaze searches mine like he's trying to read whether something has worked in my eyes.

I can only stare at him.

A ragged noise breaks the silence. I blink, my attention dropping toward it.

The other guy is struggling to reach his feet. "What… what the hell did you do to…"

He crashes to the ground, his body shaking harder.

I choke. Oh God…

Amar doesn't let go of me. His fingers digging into my arm, he pulls me with him from the stall. I stagger after him, frantically pulling my panties and skirt into place.

His hand reaches out, touching the shoulder of the guy on the floor. The man gasps, straightening like he's suddenly woken from a nightmare.

Amar keeps moving. Still hanging onto me, he marches out of the restroom, past the bar, and straight out the door. The bouncer stares but doesn't say a word.

It's not till we're back by the car that Amar stops.

"What the hell were you *doing*?" he demands, releasing me sharply.

I shiver, my arms hugging my middle. I don't respond. In the darkened parking lot, we're alone, with only a few people on the distant sidewalk who might even notice we're here.

Breathing hard, Amar turns away, running a hand over his head. "You could have—you *would have* killed him! Is that why you agreed to come here tonight? You wanted to kill somebody?"

He looks back at me like he's never seen me before, like I might be a monster, and when he speaks again, rancor drips from his tone like hot acid, burning me. "Was the idea of sleeping with me *that* terrible that you'd rather someone *died*?"

My arms tighten around my middle. "No."

"Then what the hell were you—"

"I was trying to control it."

"I was going to help you—"

"By what? Fucking me like I'm on your damn to-do list? Well, thank you *so* much, but I think I'll just—"

I cut off as he strides toward me, coming to a stop only a few inches away.

"It wasn't going to be like that." His voice is quiet. Intense. His dark eyes burn into mine.

I tremble.

He scowls, turning away. I watch while he puts several paces of distance between us.

"You don't have to do anything," he snaps. "Not if you don't want to. I was only going to do this if you thought it would help."

A breath escapes me, flabbergasted. "And what? You're just some *gigolo* who—"

"It's not about *love* with them, all right?"

I stare at him.

"Us," he corrects quietly.

He exhales, his head dropping like he's fighting hard to regain his composure.

I can't take my eyes from him. My mind is spinning. "Them," I whisper. "Amar, you said them."

He doesn't respond. He's just there, standing like he's

frozen in time, this sculpture of conflicted emotions bottled down so tight that they never get out. Not once.

Not even now.

"I should take you home," he says. "We can go by another club tomorrow. Help you take the edge off till you —" He shakes his head. "—till you decide what you want to do."

I watch him, and slowly, my arms drop to my sides. My eyes never leaving him, I cross the distance between us. I know he hears me. I don't know if he's breathing. I reach out, my hand sliding up his back to rest on his shoulder.

His eyes close, but only for a moment.

From him, it's as good as a gasp.

"We can't," he says without looking at me. "Everything has to be just like the full-bloods, Cait. There can't be anything between us."

I don't listen. Stepping around him, I keep my hand to his shoulder until I'm facing him. He doesn't meet my eyes.

My fingers reach up, touching his cheek. A breath presses from his chest like the air is being crushed from him.

"But do you want there to be?" I whisper.

His gaze goes to mine, and my lips part at what I see there. Heat. Longing. Dark, hungry desire that could devour me alive. Tingling rushes through me at the sight.

He lifts a hand to my face. His thumb brushes along my cheekbone, and his gaze tracks the motion, a look in his eyes like he's wanted to do this for a while, and then he leans down.

It's not like before, harsh and aggressive like when he found me with that other guy. Gently, his lips touch mine while his fingers slip through my hair to keep my mouth on his own. His other hand takes my back, drawing me close and pressing my breasts to his chest. His tongue twists against mine, stroking me, tangling with me, and my whole body wakes up in response. Heat pours through me, pooling in my core and making the skin between my legs throb with desire. I want this. Him. I'm so desperate for his touch that it hurts.

But he pulls away. I stare questioningly.

"Come on." He takes my hand and then steps past me, opening the passenger door.

My confusion deepens.

The corner of his mouth rises, something dark and delicious in his eyes. "Trust me."

I get in the car.

He circles around to the driver's side and climbs in. He doesn't say a word while he starts the engine.

But he glances at me, that hint of a smile still teasing at his face, and I can't help but smile in return. I have no idea what he's planning, but it almost doesn't matter.

Something's changed between us. Something more than a few words.

It's breathtaking.

⌒∾⌒

THE STREET IS DARK AND QUIET WHEN WE REACH THE apartment.

Amar holds the door for me while I get out of the car. I feel like the whole world is watching, even if no one is around us, and like my face is a cherry-red light, glowing beneath the street lamps.

I feel drawn to him like a magnet, craving the moment I can feel his hands on me again.

He shuts the door behind me and then turns. His gaze roams my face, something almost awestruck in his eyes. That tiny, secretive smile tugs at his mouth. He heads for the house.

I bite my lip and follow.

Our footsteps echo in the stairwell while we climb toward the third floor. "Your roommate going to be around tonight?" Amar whispers.

A thrill bubbles through me, so unlike what I expected to be feeling at this moment. "No."

He casts a quick glance back. I can't stop my grin at the hot, sensual promise in his eyes. When we reach the top of the steps, he takes my hand, and his thumb plays along the side of my fingers while he leads me down the hall.

Then it stops, and so does he.

My brow furrows. "Amar?"

I step closer to him and then follow his gaze.

My apartment door is ajar.

Amar starts down the hall, keeping me behind him. Every line of his body is tense. It feels like static electricity is building beneath his grip on my hand.

Cautiously, he nudges the door. It swings aside.

A breath stutters from me.

Books are scattered everywhere. The coffee table has been reduced to kindling. Chairs are overturned, and our posters have been ripped from the walls.

Amar grabs me when I try to shove by him. "Don't."

I can't tear my eyes from the room.

"Stay here." He pushes me back, watches me for a heartbeat as if to make sure I've heard him, and then inches past the door.

I trail him into the apartment anyway.

Our rooms are a wreck. I can see them through the

open doorways. My bed has been sliced open, and Ruby's too. Clothes are strewn everywhere.

"Ruby?" I call.

No answer.

"Ruby? Ruby!"

The cry bounces uselessly from the apartment walls.

"Cait." Amar takes my shoulders as if to hold me steady. "She might not have been here. She said she was going to be out tonight."

I tug my gaze in his direction only to freeze when it catches on her coat, tossed loosely amid the debris. I pull away from him and walk toward it.

There's a folded bit of paper placed on top. And next to it, her wallet and keys. With trembling fingers, I pick up the note and pull the creases of it apart. My eyes track over the words scrawled in ballpoint on the paper scrap.

We warned you.

"She was," I say, my whole body shaking. "They've taken Ruby."

PART III

14

RUBY

OF ALL THE THINGS THAT TERRIFY HER, THE WORST ARE THE screams. Wild, insane, animal screams that make her think of hyenas she saw at the zoo as a child, on one of the Redhaired Bastard's good days when he'd insisted they pretend to be a family despite the bruises they were all trying to hide. The screams cut short sometimes, the sounds becoming guttural and gurgling.

And the noises that follow…

Ruby hugs her legs tighter to her chest. They'd come from nowhere, the men who took her to this place. One moment, she'd been alone in her apartment. The next, they were there, stepping from the shadows like they'd been in them all along, grinning at her like those hyenas at the zoo. She'd had no time to scream before they were already on her, smothering the world with their white handkerchief of chloroform and hefting her up to take her who knew where. She'd only seen them start to tear the apartment to pieces before everything went black.

She woke here, in this rusted steel cage with its thick bars and its ceiling too short to stand beneath. Heavy locks secure the door, so strong they look capable of withstanding a rhinoceros. The floor of the cage is concrete, as is the ground beyond, and a tiny drain is the only feature in the cell. Red-brown flakes cling to its metal grating. She tries not to think of why.

Footsteps sound on the walkway beyond the bars. There are other cages here. Possibly other prisoners too. Most of the cells are empty, though sometimes she thinks she sees something moving deep within the shadows. She doesn't know where the screams come from. Finding out almost seems like it might be the most terrible thing of all.

A figure comes into view below the utilitarian strip light that is the only illumination in this place. He's huge; maybe one of the people who took her, maybe somebody else altogether. Over his clothes, he wears a rubber smock and thick boots like a farmer in a slaughterhouse, and the pale skin of his bald head shines under the strip light, revealing long and puckered scars. His eyes are so colorless, they're almost white. She can't see anything sane in their gaze.

Another guy walks up behind him. Her breath catches, reality spinning. "Kyle?"

He barely even looks at her. "Break it," he says to the other man.

"It's dense," the man replies. His voice is cultured and nothing like his appearance. "Powerful. To get through it—"

"Yeah, yeah," Kyle interrupts. "The Legacy bitch obviously dumped everything she had into creating a Protection this strong. Now **break it.***"*

The man bends down, unbolts the lock. She scrambles to the back of the cage on instinct, but he doesn't care. With long arms, he reaches in, snagging her ankle and then dragging her forward. She cries out, grabbing at the bars. "What are you doing? Kyle, please, what the hell—"

A sizzling sensation rockets over her body, like every nerve ending has woken after having gone numb. She shrieks while it builds, crackling over her skin, burning from her toes to her scalp.

The large man grunts as if in discomfort. His lips pull back, baring his teeth in a rictus of pain. The electric feeling reaches a crescendo around her, and he snarls as it does, a heartbeat before the sensation seems to fly apart like a firecracker.

The tingling fades. She feels strange. Somehow naked, though she can't figure out why.

Ragged breaths leave the large man, and sweat drips from his face. He doesn't release her. She can feel him shaking. "Done," he growls.

Gasping, she looks back to find Kyle watching her.

His mouth curls into a smile. There's nothing in his eyes. "Excellent. Then let's begin."

15

"CAIT?"

Amar's words come from the distance, far away and small compared to the note in my hand.

"Cait." Hands grasp my shoulders. A gasping breath enters my lungs. I look up to see Amar's dark eyes staring into my own.

With a shaking hand, I extend the note to him. His eyes flick down to it and then swiftly return to me like I matter far more to him than the scrap of paper. "*Who* took Ruby?" he asks.

My mouth moves as I try to find the words. My life is madness. Now it's stolen my best friend in the world.

"V-Volgert. Has to be. Kyle, he… the other day, he threatened—"

A noise from outside ends my words. My eyes snap toward the hallway.

"What the—" sputters one of the guys who lives next door. Footsteps come toward the apartment.

Amar doesn't waste a second. His grasp tightening on

my shoulder, he throws a fast look around the apartment and then pulls me with him toward the ruins of my bedroom. In the shadows, piles of blankets from my bed and drawers of clothes clutter the floor, but we don't make it that far. At the point where the light from the living room ends, the air changes around us, and then the apartment is gone. Darkness surrounds us, rushing with wisp-like fog, and with it comes a shock of cold that fades a second after it begins.

My next step lands me on a patio overlooking the city. We're hundreds of feet up, with the lights of the town spread out in the darkness below us. The balcony itself is floored with polished granite and surrounded by a steel railing with glass panels in between the support bars. Light pours through windows behind me, the glow ending just to my left, and when I turn, I see we're standing outside Bianca's penthouse apartment.

Amar drops his hand from me quickly, and despite everything, the action hurts. He's back to that now, I guess. Hiding everything. Not letting anyone see a hint of emotion.

Especially not the ones he showed in that parking lot outside Temptation.

"Come on," he says, his voice tight. He starts toward the sliding glass door, not looking at me.

A cold wind sweeps around me, cutting through the thin fabric of my emerald-green dress—*Ruby's* emerald-green dress—and chilling my bare shoulders and legs. Hugging my arms close, I trail after him.

Warmer air surrounds me when I enter the apartment, bringing with it heady scents I can't place. Incense maybe. Sandalwood or vanilla or something. The two Dobermans are where we left them, resting on their cushions by the windows like the dogs have been installed there. Flames snap and dance in the fireplace on the far-right wall. Two champagne glasses have been left in front of them, one of which is stained with rose lipstick.

Amar mutters a curse under his breath. "Bianca?"

Silence follows for a moment, and then I hear rustling from the second floor. Bianca appears at the top of the stairway, a black, silken sheet held around her body and incredulity on her face. Her blonde waves are tousled, and her skin is flushed. "What? Amar, I'm kind of busy here."

"Bianca?" comes a male voice from down the hall. "Is everything all right?"

"Just a second," she calls back sweetly. Her brow rises at Amar.

"We need your help," he states. "It's an emergency."

Bianca stares at him like she's trying to decide whether to care. "What is it?" she says finally.

He pauses. "Who's upstairs?"

"Just *tell* me."

"Houses. Her friend. Trouble."

Bianca's mouth tightens, and I can just read the expression. She's going to say something snarky. Something careless, and then she'll tell us to leave. Ruby's *life* is in danger, and this cold-hearted bitch—

A sensation like static tingles over my skin.

Amar's attention snaps to me. "Cait."

His hand returns to my shoulder. A sharp breath enters my lungs at the contact, and the static falters.

He looks up at Bianca. The girl's jaw muscles jump.

"Fine." She bites off the word and then spins and stalks back down the hall.

Amar doesn't take his hand away this time. "Cait," he repeats more softly. "We will find Ruby. Just breathe."

I look up at him. His fingers tighten on my shoulder like he's trying to will me into believing him.

"—family emergency."

Bianca's voice comes from upstairs. She sounds so much warmer than I've ever heard her.

Amar's hand drops away from me again. My chest clenches. I feel like a yo-yo, yanked back and forth by how much better I feel when he's touching me and how much it hurts when that goes away.

A guy with messy blond hair emerges from the hallway upstairs. He's not wearing a shirt, and even from the first floor, it's easy to see all his muscles. His biceps are big enough to be cantaloupes. His torso is hairless, chiseled with countless muscles of its own. He probably spends more time at the gym than I do at my job. His jeans hang low around his hips, and it occurs to me he might not be wearing any underwear, given how much of his skin I—

I end the thought fast, looking away.

"Who's this?" the guy asks.

My eyes flick back up to find Bianca coming from the hallway. She's replaced the sheet with a pink satin gown that ends at her thighs. "Friends. Listen, I'm really sorry, but—"

"Do you want me to come with you to the hospital?" he interrupts, concern in his voice.

"Oh, that's so *sweet* of you. No, I'm sure my brother will be fine. Probably just a false alarm."

He nods while he descends the steps. Bianca follows him only to stop when he pauses at the front door. "Call you?" he prompts.

She smiles gratefully and rises to her tiptoes to give him a kiss. "So sweet," she repeats. I swear a blush is creeping across her cheeks.

He returns the smile and closes the door behind him when he leaves.

The affectionate expression vanishes from Bianca's face immediately. Making an exasperated noise, she strides back into the living room. "Honestly, Amar. Do you have any idea the *stamina* that gorgeous idiot probably had? I could've gotten enough energy to last me a *month* after—"

"So call him later," Amar cuts in, a touch heatedly.

She tosses him a withering look. Reaching the couch, she drops onto the white cushions and regards us both tiredly. "Now *what* happened?"

"Cait thinks Volgert took her friend."

"And is Cait *right*?"

Shivers course through me. Amar's eyes twitch to me like he's checking to make sure I won't explode.

"I think so," he allows, a heavy note of caution in his tone. "They made it look like a break-in, but they left the girl's things with a message on top of them. Seems they wanted a grand gesture Linden couldn't dismiss and to make sure Cait got their point at the same time."

Bianca makes an irritated noise. "Yeah, well, I'm sorry, but I don't—"

Static surges over me, and a vase on a nearby table shatters.

Fear spikes through my rage, and I'm shaking so hard I can't breathe. Holy shit, I just… I have no idea what I just did.

Again.

The others don't appear nearly as shocked, though. At least, not in the same way. From their post near the window, the Dobermans let out a warning growl, but Amar and Bianca only stare at me, concerned and disgusted respectively.

"*Excuse* me," Bianca protests. "Don't just come in here and break my—"

"Bianca, shut up." Amar takes my hand. "Cait, *stop*. You need to—"

I pull away from him. I know what he's going to say, and I won't do it. I don't want to calm down. I'm sick to my stomach over calming down. "How can she help?" I demand of Amar. "How can this selfish, useless, stuck-up bitch *ever* help!"

My words end in a shriek. I can't feel my hands. My feet. Everything is pounding and racing and tingling and…

I stride toward the door. I don't need them. I'll find Ruby myself. Figure out how to get in touch with that sick bastard Kyle and—

My footsteps stop, an image of the destroyed apartment flashing through my mind. Get in touch with…

Oh my God, I can't believe I didn't think of it.

I scramble for my phone. My stupid, crap phone that I always have with me.

And Ruby always has hers too. It wasn't in the apartment, though. Her keys, her wallet, her whole fucking life was there.

But not that.

I hear footsteps behind me.

"Cait?" Amar tries carefully.

I don't respond. With shaking hands, I fumble through the security code and then find Ruby's number.

"What are you doing?" Amar persists.

"She has her cell," I tell him, willing the statement to be true. "It wasn't at the apartment." I touch the icon to put the call through.

Amar comes up beside me. "Speakerphone," he says, the words gentle and an order all at the same time.

I look up at him and then do what he said. The ringing sound fills the entryway. By the steps leading down to the living room, Bianca leans on the railing, watching us both.

The ringing stops.

"Well," Kyle comments on the other end. "I was wondering when I'd hear from you."

"*Where is she?*"

He chuckles. My fingers clench around the phone.

"Why don't you come meet me, and we can talk about that?"

My heart pounds. "Tell me where she is."

"Ah now, Cait, you know that's not how this works. Come meet me. Alone. Intersection of Hitchson and Crowsfield Road. Half an hour."

"Kyle, you—"

He chuckles again and then hangs up.

A shuddering breath leaves me. My fingers crush around the plastic case of my phone, my knuckles turning white.

Carefully, Amar puts a hand over the cell and takes it away like he anticipates me dropping it. Maybe throwing it. And he might be right. My whole body is trembling. The world feels like it's spinning around me, and on some level, I just want to scream.

I look up at him.

He's watching me. After a moment, I can see the argument fade from his eyes. Grimacing slightly, he hands the phone back to me and twitches his chin toward the door, his gaze never leaving mine.

"All right," he says. "Let's go."

When we reach our destination, there isn't any discussion of Amar staying in the car. Tense as a thread about to snap, I follow him away from the sedan we borrowed from Bianca, since Amar's vehicle is still at my apartment. The night is eerily quiet. The two gravel roads stretch away from each other, a single, ancient streetlamp marking their crossing while, around us, fields and farms sleep in the darkness. We're miles from town, though a faint glow from beyond the hills marks where I know the city waits. I haven't seen another car this entire time.

I fight back a surge of anger while I scan the darkness. Demons meeting at a crossroads. Kyle clearly has a flair for the dramatic—the bastard.

"Now, I *thought* I told you to come alone."

My heart shoots up my throat, and I whirl. Standing at the edge of the dim glow cast by the aging streetlamp, Kyle regards me with a cocksure grin.

"And you really expected she'd do that," Amar replies,

his tone utterly level. He could be commenting on the color of the gravel or the fact there are stars in the sky.

Kyle chuckles. Two huge guys are at his side, suit-clad like the Linden henchmen who'd grabbed me off the street. "Maybe not," Kyle acknowledges. "Though I am interested to see *you* here, Amar. Getting involved in anything to do with the Houses…" He makes a tsking noise. "How utterly *unexpected* of you."

Intrigue drips from his tone, as if there's a universe of meaning behind the words.

Amar's face goes subzero in response. "What do you want?"

Kyle smiles. "Nothing much. Cait's help."

I shiver when he turns that cat-with-a-trapped-mouse gaze on me. "Where's Ruby?" I demand.

"Oh, Ruby's not on the table. The Touched are a resource, after all—as your boss is *certainly* aware." He smirks like he's told a joke. "I'm not going to waste one now that I have her. I only wanted to make sure I got your attention since you seem to have ignored me the first time around."

My shivering spreads through my core at his words and how they confirm my fears. Touched. They're turning her into…

With effort, I force myself to stay focused. "What's that supposed to mean?"

"House Linden. You haven't passed my message to them. Or maybe they didn't listen. Either way, there are consequences for that kind of rudeness."

"I don't work for Linden. I—"

"Oh, please. You spoke with Alistair himself only moments after seeing me."

I stare at him. "How do you know that?"

Kyle gives me an amused look. "How do you think?"

"Spies," Amar supplies coldly.

Kyle dips his head to the side in tacit acknowledgment. "Among other things, sure. But your boss seems to have missed the point, so let me make this clear. The Protected are only the beginning. A warning. But for every day House Linden doesn't give us what we want, more of their people will disappear. Next one's up in—" Kyle glances to the enormous guy on his left, who extends a watch-bound wrist. "Oh, let's say thirteen hours. That's a fun number." He grins at me. "Linden can't protect its own, Cait, no matter *what* resources they have on their side. I know that. Now so do you. So explain it to them, will you? And make it soon."

He turns, heading toward the shadows.

"Give Ruby back," I snap. "You want my help, give—"

Kyle scoffs, glancing over his shoulder to me. "God, Cait. Little suggestion, one Legacy to another? Get a handle on that human side of you. It's unbecoming. I warned you what could happen to Ruby. It did. Now be a good little Linden bitch, and go back and tell your master to listen this time, eh?"

He winks at me and then turns at the edge of the light's glow. He and the other men vanish.

I stride after him. It's not like I have a plan. I don't even know how to follow. It's just instinct.

Or maybe outrage.

Amar grabs my arm, stopping me. "Don't."

I rip it away. "We have to—"

"They'll have safeguards around wherever they've gone to make sure no one can track them. Trust me." He scowls. "We'll find her a different way."

I stare at him, and I have no idea what to do. I want to argue. Hell, I want to scream. "We have to go to Linden."

"That won't fix this."

"But Alistair offered to help me. Keep people safe." My stomach turns even while I say the words. They aren't exactly true. Alistair *had* offered to help me. Hell, he'd offered to make me Cait of House Linden or whatever. But in exchange, he'd wanted me to be his prostitute. To sleep with whomever he ordered me to, in cases that "needed persuasion."

But if it saves Ruby…

Amar shakes his head. "Alistair won't care about Ruby any more than that guy did. Please, Cait, we can do this another way. Let me talk to Bianca—"

"*Bianca?*"

"She—"

"Bianca won't help me, Amar. You saw her tonight."

"She will. Give me the chance to convince her."

I look away. That could take forever. So is this, for that matter. We shouldn't even be *having* this argument, not with Ruby still out there and those bastards doing who knew what to her. We don't have the time.

"I'm going to Linden."

"Cait—"

"Alistair said he'd keep the people I care about safe, and I'm sorry, Amar, but that's a damn sight better than *hoping* Bianca decides to—"

"She *will help*, Cait. Please. You can't—"

I turn and head for the car. I don't want to listen to this.

"He'll make you kill for him."

I stop.

"The 'persuasion' he talked about," Amar continues. "It's murder. He'll send you to people who matter to his enemies, and he'll order you to sleep with them and drain them till they die. Volgert isn't the only House that uses others as leverage."

I hear his footsteps on the rough ground behind me.

"But Bianca has contacts," Amar finishes. "So do I. And with their help, we will tear the city apart, and we will find Ruby. I promise."

I don't move. My eyes are locked on the fields and hills and the distant glow of Corvinson on the horizon. And in all of it, there's no answer. Nothing I can do to make this better. I feel helpless, trapped in a nightmare where every terrible thing possible keeps happening like some cruel and endless joke.

And I can't seem to wake up.

My eyes close. I'm shaking all over. All I want to do is start running for the city right now, if only that would bring Ruby home faster.

"Please, Cait," Amar urges.

Jerkily, I manage a nod.

"Thank you," he says quietly.

I can't respond. His footsteps crunch on the gravel as he walks toward the sedan. Struggling not to feel like I'm failing Ruby, I trail him away from the crossroads.

17

I'M SITTING ON A BED, HOURS LATER, TOO ANXIOUS TO EVEN pace the room.

And we still haven't found Ruby.

I adjust my grip on the edge of the white duvet. My fingers are bloodless. Cramped too. My dress is gone, replaced by a pair of too-tight jeans from Bianca and a blouse. It's pink. I think the color is the only one she owns. Muted light from the hall lamp slips through the space where the door has been left ajar, while a pale glow from the city comes through the windows behind me. Bianca grudgingly offered me the room after Amar brought us back to her apartment. She's downstairs now, ostensibly calling her contacts in an effort to find Ruby while Amar is doing the same.

And I'm here, doing nothing.

My hands quiver. It's nearly three in the morning. On a normal day, I'd be waking up in a few hours to go to work at the library.

The thought prompts a breath of a laugh, nothing

funny in the sound. Things haven't been normal in what feels like ages and has probably only been a week.

That thought just hurts.

A shadow blocks the dim light from the hall. My breath catching, I look up.

"Cait?" Amar pushes the door aside. "I thought you were going to get some sleep."

I almost want to laugh again. Like that was ever going to happen. "You guys find anything?"

He hesitates. "Not yet. Bianca's still making calls."

I exhale, my eyes burning with angry, futile tears.

By the doorway, Amar doesn't move, and then his eyes slide to the hallway like he's weighing something. His jaw tightening briefly, he considers a moment longer and then steps inside and eases the door shut behind him, sealing out the light.

I hear the lock click. I watch him, wary and confused.

He crosses the room and sinks down in front of me. His hand reaches up, wrapping around one of my own, and then he stops. "You're freezing."

Straightening quickly, he walks over to the closet and pulls a blanket from inside. Unfurling it, he drapes the woven cotton around my shoulders and then crouches down in front of me again. His hands take mine through the blanket.

I look away. I want to draw back. I want to shout. But it's not like that'll accomplish anything, and I'm not quite willing to end the contact in any case.

"We will find her, Cait," he insists gently.

I nod because it's the polite thing to do. The kind thing. I don't believe him, though. Not really. They've had hours.

I should have gone to see Alistair.

The thought makes me feel sick. I can't be a prostitute for that man. I can't *kill* people.

Amar could be wrong.

My gut doesn't believe that for a second.

"Cait," Amar says, and I hear something hard in his voice, like he's reading whatever expression is on my face. Like he knows where my thoughts are going. "You're not still thinking of talking to Alistair, are you?"

I open my mouth. The lie won't come.

He lets out a breath. "You have to give us time."

I don't look back at him. Time. Volgert could be turning my best friend into one of those Touched things right now.

My hands are shaking.

From the corner of my eye, I see his lids close briefly. "Listen, I get that she's your friend. But you can't seriously be willing to *murder* people to—"

I push away from the bed and put several steps of distance between us. I don't need to explain myself to him.

"I'm not trying to upset you," he says.

An angry noise leaves me, harsh and raw.

He hesitates at the sound. "Cait, I just—"

"You don't get it."

"No. No, I don't. You can't play around with people like Alistair. Not when it comes to *killing*—"

"What if it were your sister? Your mom?"

His expression makes my stomach quiver. He looks deadly.

I force myself to press onward. "Ruby matters to me, Amar, okay? Like that, she matters to me."

"Why?"

I stare at him. How the hell is it his business *why*? The prying bastard, because she *does*, that's why! Who asks a question like that?

Realization spreads over me. He's a demon. Born human, sure, but he grew up here. In this. Their culture, their world. For God's sake, one of his closest friends is a bitch who saved him from the Houses only because he was a "curiosity" to her. He actually might not get how anyone could care this much about somebody who isn't blood.

I feel sick. Every time I turn around, their fucked-up world is smacking me in the face.

"Why are you helping me?" I ask.

He appears thrown by the question.

"You barely know me," I persist. "We only met a few days ago. But you came with me tonight to see Kyle. You brought me to meet Bianca. You even showed up on my doorstep after Alistair's people yanked me off the street." An ache throbs in my chest, a futile pain at how close Amar and I came to... to *something*. I pull the blanket tighter around my shoulders, trying to ward it off. "I-I know what you said in the parking lot outside Temptation, about them and us and... and I don't know what... But if you can't understand why I would want to help my friend, then why the hell are you helping me?"

His expression starts to close down again. Go all guarded in that way he has. "You need it."

"So does Ruby."

"Yes, but—"

"You're telling me if Bianca was out there right now, possibly being tortured into *insanity*, you wouldn't be doing whatever it took to find her?"

He tenses further. I can't read anything from his face. "Bianca's father would destroy half the city if that happened."

I scoff. "Okay, well, goodie for him. But Ruby's not that lucky, so I'm not leaving her out there, all right? Whatever it takes, I'm *not*. Ruby's watched out for me. She…" I close my eyes briefly, regrouping. I can't finish that sentence.

"She what?"

I shiver. "She never should have been my friend, okay? But she is. I'm not letting her pay with her life for that fact."

He looks confused. "Why shouldn't she have been your friend?"

"Doesn't matter. That's not the point."

"Cait, come on. You want me to understand why you'd be willing to murder innocent people for this girl, then—"

I make an infuriated noise. "I'm not saying I'm willing to—*God*, I just—"

"Then explain this to me."

"Where the hell do you get off *demanding* that I—"

His expression turns exasperated, and he heads for the door. Adrenaline spikes through my chest. Fucking idiot, me. He's the only help in this that I've got.

"Amar," I protest.

He looks back, and I can't figure out what to say. How to fix this.

"You don't know me," he states, his voice tight and quiet. "And you're right, I don't know you either. So whatever you do is your business." He turns toward the door again.

"Please."

He stops.

A ragged breath leaves me. I can't talk about this. I *never* talk about what happened back then—for her sake as much as mine.

But sometimes, some promises have to get broken.

My eyes squeeze shut briefly, as if to crush this all away. "I'll try, okay?"

He hesitates and then drops his hand from the door handle. Watching me, he crosses the room and sits down on the edge of the bed. His brow twitches up, waiting.

I swallow hard. I can do this. If I focus, if I'm *careful*, I can get through this, and no one gets hurt.

Least of all me.

Drawing a breath, I cross the room to join him. I sink down to the edge of the mattress, leaving distance between us.

His mouth tightens, but he doesn't say anything.

"Ruby and I met when we were sixteen," I tell him. "I'd known *of* her for a couple years before that—she was one of the most popular girls in my school—but we'd never spoken. I was…" I frown. "I had a hard time with the people at school. But in my spare time, I did volunteer work. Good way to stay away from home and all that. And one of my volunteer places was the local homeless shelter."

I take a breath, working to keep myself focused. "That's where I ended up seeing her. Ruby's dad… he, uh… he was an alcoholic. Pretty abusive. Physically, verbally…" I shake my head, remembering what I'd overheard at the shelter. What Ruby told me as years went on. "The Redhaired Bastard, she calls him. But one night, he came home, and well, he kicked them out. Ruby, her mom, her siblings. Just shoved them out onto the street and said he was bringing his new girlfriend to live there instead. It was a huge mess—cops, Child Services, all that—and her family had nowhere to go, so they ended up at the shelter."

I shift on the edge of the bed, my mind flashing back to the moment I saw her there. The look on her face when she spotted me too, fierce challenge undercut by fear. The way she drew herself up like she was getting ready for a fight while her younger siblings clung to her even more than to their mother.

Always the protective one, Ruby. Even of me.

I struggle to push the memories aside, but it's difficult. Other things want to rise up and make me remember them too.

"The thing is," I press on. "Kids can be pretty cruel. And Ruby, she spent years hiding what her life was like. So when I saw her there, I think she was afraid I'd use it against her. Try to scavenge some scrap of popularity at her expense or something. But..." I shrug. "Talk about a terrible thing to do, right? Feeding her to the wolves like that, especially when her situation wasn't all that different from mine. I mean, my stepmother is a *nightmare.* If not for my dad, she would have thrown me out on the street *years* ago, and even he couldn't stop Arlene from making my life so bad that by that point I was ready to just—" I look away, clamming up fast.

"To just what?" Amar asks quietly.

Tears sting my eyes. Damn me. I'd intended to have this conversation *around* that detail, not run right into it five seconds after I opened my mouth.

"Cait?"

"Nothing. It was just bad. But Ruby, she, um—"

"To just *what*, Cait?" His voice is harder. Edgy, like somehow he suspects what I'm trying to avoid.

And dammit, it's not fair. He doesn't have any right to know.

Even if I'm not sure what to do about that now. Continuing to insist it was nothing probably won't get me far, and telling him to mind his own business…

I'll drive away the only person helping me.

My stomach twists. I don't want to talk about this. I can feel his tension, though. It's like heat waves pounding at me, growing stronger by the second.

A scowl tugs at my face. "I... I was going to kill myself."

His whole body seems to go still.

I swallow. "I didn't want to deal with it anymore. Arlene. My life. It felt like there was no way out, like there'd never *be* any way out, and I just... I hated myself for it. I wanted it to stop. Everything and how much it hurt. So I snuck into the girls' bathroom at school, waited till classes started and..." My stomach churns at the memories. The tiny pocket knife in my hand. The cold resolution, and how all my tears dried up into an eerie, shivering calm.

I draw a rough breath. "Ruby found me. Seems crazy, I know. Like, what the hell, right? But she'd decided to talk to me that day. She'd seen me go into the girls' restroom before class, and when I didn't come back out, she followed me. She found me right before I... right before I did it."

My shoulders roll as if to shrug off the memory. "She stopped me. Talked to me. She'd come to ask why I didn't tell anyone about her, and by the time we left that stupid bathroom..." I shake my head. "Things got better after that. I swore to her I'd never tell anyone about her dad, and she swore she'd try to help me out. Make high school suck less. And she did. Stuff there got better, and home just... It felt like there was a light at the end of the tunnel. Like good was out there somewhere." I look over at him. "Ruby saved my life, Amar. That's why I can't let anyone threaten hers."

He doesn't say anything, not for the longest time. He

simply sits there, his gaze on my hands, and I try not to fidget, worrying he's picturing what almost happened that day, worrying about what he might think of me now.

"I'm sorry," he says quietly.

I shift a bit. I can't stop myself.

His dark gaze rises. Searches over my face. "Ruby wouldn't want you to give up your own life, though. I know I don't know her, but…" His brow shrugs like he's sure of his words anyway.

I look down.

"I have people out, searching," he continues. "People who *will* find her. And Bianca and her brother do too. Their family may be neutrals, but they have connections throughout the demon world. That's why I wanted to bring you to meet her. I know she doesn't seem like it—" A scoff leaves him. "Hell, I know she acts like a heartless bitch most of the time, but she's actually one of the best people I've ever met. If she promises she'll help you—and she has—she'll follow through to the end. Trust me on that."

I hesitate. Everything I've seen of Bianca is so different from what he describes.

And yet…

"Okay," I agree softly.

"Thank you."

I glance up at him. Amar is studying me. His hand moves, taking my own carefully like he's afraid I'll pull away. And I freeze. The look in his eyes… it's like I'm all he sees. Me, now. Me, then, back in that restroom, alone in the moments before Ruby walked in. But there's no pity in his gaze. Just something else, dark and deep.

Safety.

I can't breathe. My thoughts are trying to catch up to

my impressions, struggling to put words to a man so unfathomable it should be funny. I don't know what he wants, though. To kiss me? To have sex? Somewhere inside, I'm still ready for that, but that part of me feels like it's drowning in the nightmare of this evening, the exhaustion of all the hours since, and the rawness of what I've just said.

He lifts his other hand, taking my cheek, and his thumb strays across my lips, parting them while his eyes track the motion. My heart slams into my ribs. Even the simple contact makes my insides start to burn. Maybe I'm drowning in all this madness.

Maybe I just need something good to hang onto.

But he lets me go. A breath escapes him, frustration in the sound, and his hand leaves my cheek at the same moment his gaze falls from mine. "You should get some sleep."

I blink in surprise. "What?"

His eyes skirt toward the door. "It's late. I'll come wake you if we hear anything."

"But… what about you?" I sputter as he rises to his feet. "Don't you need sleep? You could… I mean, if you wanted to stay here…?"

"I can't."

"But—"

"It's complicated. I—" He grimaces. "Please, just get some sleep."

An incredulous noise leaves me as he pulls open the door. "Amar?"

For a moment, he looks back, his eyes lingering on me, and I can't tell what I'm seeing. Regret? I almost feel like I'm wishing it into existence. He's standing there like a sculpture, motionless and cold, nothing but untouchable rock all the way through. And I can't figure out what to say. I don't get this, why he pulled away without any warning. Bianca made this big deal about demons not wanting anything to do with love, but for God's sake, surely that doesn't mean he can't be *nice* for more than a few minutes at a time?

"I'll let you know if we hear anything." He repeats the words like a promise.

And then he's gone.

18

I END UP FALLING ASLEEP IN A TANGLE OF THE COTTON blanket Amar put around me, and when I open my eyes, I feel like a frown has permanently etched itself onto my face. I still can't believe him. The Laws of Nature should be against anyone going from hot to cold that fast.

My bleary gaze finds the alarm clock on the nightstand. It's been four hours. The sun is coming up.

And neither Amar nor Bianca have come to find me.

My frustration boils higher. I tug myself free of the shrink-wrap of blanket and sit up. Screw this. Bianca was against it last night, but maybe I can still help make calls and move this along faster.

I shove up from the bed. Raking my fingers through my hair, I head to the door and tug it open forcibly before I start into the hall.

Only to freeze.

"—the hell is *wrong* with you?" Bianca demands, her voice carrying from the first floor.

Amar's response is too low to make out. Straining to hear, I creep toward the end of the hallway.

"Seriously, Amar," Bianca continues more softly, like he's told her to keep it down. "I get forming an alliance with another neutral, all right? I do. It's strategic, and up till about five *seconds* ago, it made sense. But this is *bullshit*. Let me call Brett again. See if—"

"He said it'd take hours to hear back from his contacts."

"*So*? How does that justify risking yourself like this?"

Alarm shoots through me. Wait, what's he doing?

I inch closer to the stairwell opening.

"I'm not," Amar says, his voice carefully restrained. "These two are neutrals. They won't—"

"And if Volgert finds out you're involved in this? Oh *wait*, they already did, thanks to your little field trip last night! *God*, Amar, do you honestly think Lucretia is just going to *let* you—"

Bianca cuts off, but nothing follows. I don't even breathe.

Footsteps sound on the stairs.

"Eavesdropping's pretty damn rude, you know," she snaps, her voice coming from beyond the hallway exit.

I hesitate and then walk out to the landing. On the first floor, Amar is standing beside the glass dining table, his jacket already on and his hand holding his cell phone like I caught him midway to tucking it into a pocket.

"What's going on?" I ask.

"Nothing," he says. "Sorry for waking you."

The words are so calm, it's like what I heard never even happened. My temper starts to rise again. "Where are you going?"

"Just to get information. I'll let you know if it leads to Ruby."

"And what? I stay here?" I don't look toward Bianca. I don't need to. Amar might think she's a good person, but I can still feel the derision rolling off of her in waves. "No, I'm coming too."

Amar pauses. "It's not necessary."

I march down the stairs, past him, and snag my sandals from beside the door. They're strappy and ridiculous, a holdover from my outfit for the club last night, but they're the only thing I have. I don't look down at my borrowed clothes, so rumpled from sleep they probably look like they spent a year at the bottom of a drawer. "Let's go."

"Cait, you don't—"

I stride toward the elevator. I hear Bianca scoff behind me.

Amar follows. He doesn't say a word when the elevator arrives, and once we're inside, I lock my gaze on the doors.

The dull thrum of machinery is the only sound.

"The people we're going to meet," he starts, his voice so flat that it's chilling, "they may act strangely. Say odd things. Just… stay quiet. Let me ask the questions."

There's barely a request in his tone.

"Who are we meeting?" I retort.

"A couple people from out of town. They have a business arrangement with the Houses, which means they may know where Ruby's being held."

"Business arrangement?"

"Yes."

We arrive at the garage. Amar strides from the elevator toward Bianca's black sedan without another word.

I exhale, my jaw working around. I want to press him for more. Demand he tell me what the hell is going on.

I don't even know where to begin.

Scowling, I hurry across the garage.

The car ride is as silent as the elevator, and when we pull up next to a dock by the Puloxi River, Amar still doesn't say anything. Pushing open his car door, he climbs from the sedan and leaves me to follow.

My scowl deepens. I shove open the door and get out.

The air is moist and cool, and it clings to my skin while we walk toward the river. Sunlight glints off the water, pink and gold and soft in the way only early morning hours can pull off. A boat is docked ahead of us—a vaguely boxy structure like a floating RV, only bigger and with porches at either end. A patio runs the length of the roof as well, surrounded by railings. Though windows line the cream-and-blue-striped walls, the glass is darkened, so I can't see a hint of what's inside.

Amar walks up to the edge of the dock and stops by the foot of the gangplank leading to the deck. I come up beside him, glancing from him to the boat and wondering what we're waiting for.

The door ahead of us opens. A man grins at us from within the shelter of the boat. "Well, hey. Come on in."

He steps back and motions toward the space behind him. Amar's expression doesn't change while he starts up the walkway. Torn between uncertainty and impatience, I trail after him.

The smell of incense and fried eggs hits me, jarring against each other like I've walked into a New-Age breakfast joint. The boat's interior continues that impression. It's nothing like the outside. Gold light comes from a pair of miniature chandeliers on the ceiling, both of which sway with the gentle rocking of the boat. Patterned with some kind of textured mosaic, the ceiling is colored like oil-slicked brass, and the surface reflects the chandelier light with shades like a peacock. The walls are paneled with glossy golden wood, interrupted only by windows muffled behind maroon velvet curtains. Persian rugs cover the floor, layered one over the other, and my feet sink into them when I leave the doorway. The seating is a mix of red and gold as well, dotted with satiny decorative pillows with tassels hanging from their ends.

I feel like I've walked into a floating version of a hippie's wagon.

The guy in front of me doesn't do much to make me reconsider the description. With baggy jeans, a colorful linen shirt that hangs open in a V below his neck, and a brown vest stitched in a zigzag all around its hem, he looks like he stepped from Woodstock straight onto this boat. His dark hair is tied back with a suede thong into a long ponytail, and his feet are bare. He isn't alone either. A young woman lies on one of the seats, her arm tucked behind her head and her legs curled up on the cushions. Her brunette waves are twisted into a loose ponytail, and she has striking blue eyes the same shade as a summer sky. She's wearing ripped jean shorts and a striped tank top that leaves her slender midriff bare. An empty plate dotted by egg bits rests on the end table beside her while, in her free hand, she's holding a Bloody Mary.

She grins at us around the bright-green straw in her glass. "Hey there."

I manage a smile and then look quickly to Amar, trying to judge what to do.

He's as difficult to read as ever. A surge of irritation goes through me despite everything. Stay quiet, he'd said. No questions.

Be nice if he could give me some help here, though.

"Bianca said you had information for us?" Amar responds evenly.

The guy shakes his head. "Goddess, you're uptight, man. Sit down, eh? Who's your friend?"

Amar pauses, and then he gestures for me to precede him over to a low couch against the far wall. I cross the narrow room and sink onto the velvet fabric. The seat gives awkwardly beneath me, tipping me back against the maroon cushions and making me appear far more relaxed than I actually feel. Amar lowers himself to the couch, beside me. He never looks at me once.

"An associate of Bianca's," he replies. "Now, where are they?"

The guy glances to the girl and then returns his attention to Amar. "Why's it so crucial that you find them?"

"That's not important."

He snorts. "Okay, well, what's your plan?"

"Also not important."

The girl scoffs. "It is if we end up in trouble with a House."

Amar is silent.

She puts her drink on an end table and sits up. "You know why we're here, right? What they've brought us in for? This set is going to be *huge*. They're talking, like, twenty at a minimum. They'll be furious if anyone screws that up."

My brow flickers down. Set? Twenty?

"We're only after one," Amar replies.

My confusion scarcely fades. One. And twenty. People, then. And a set is…?

"Yeah, well," the girl counters. "They'll still be pissed. Look, I'm not saying Leaf here was wrong to talk to that Chastain girl, but if you have to come to us to find out when the set even *is*, let alone anything else…" She glances at the guy briefly. "The Houses obviously aren't allowing any of their folk to talk to you, so what's this about?"

Amar seems to consider for a moment. His eyes almost, but don't quite, go to me. "One of Volgert's Touched owes me money. Something happens to them, I can't get what I need in order to collect. Simple as that."

His voice is ice. It sends shivers through me.

Leaf just laughs. *"Money?* Man, you're fucking with House business for *that?"*

"My problem, not yours."

"Well, *yeah*, but…" Leaf shrugs, still chuckling.

"Where is Volgert keeping them?"

Leaf hesitates, shifting around like he's reconsidering. "Eh, I don't know." He nods toward the girl. "I mean, Blue has a point. If things get screwed up—"

"I only need the information."

"Doesn't matter," Blue interjects before Leaf can speak. "Listen, I know that plenty of our kind wouldn't have an issue with this, but Leaf and I view our job as a mission. *Money* isn't worth jeopardizing that. If the Houses find out we helped you learn about their set, they might pull our deal. And then there's going to be a whole lot of Touched whom we can't feed off of and put out of their misery."

My brow shoots up. Wait, *what?* "You feed off the Touched?" I sputter.

Amar glances at me, visibly urging me to shut up.

Leaf laughs. "Uh, yeah? Damn, girl, you think you'd never heard of the Houses' deal with vampires before."

My body goes cold. Vampires. The guy just said vampires.

And I don't think he's joking even the *tiniest* bit.

My gaze flies to the thickly curtained windows and the

utter lack of light that slips past them. To the plate with its debris of fried eggs, so incongruous now. To the Bloody Mary beside it.

Oh my God, I wonder if that's actually—

"It's a mercy," Blue says firmly.

Her words yank my focus back to her. She's watching me with an electric intensity to her pale eyes.

"We feed on the ones who are about to die," she continues. "Give them peace after everything they've already suffered, so their lives don't end in agony."

I stare at her. Mercy. Vampires feeding is a—

The rest of the words register on me. The ones who are about to die. "*What?*"

"Where are the Touched?" Amar interjects, his tone hard.

The girl watches me for another moment and then turns to him. "I told you. Not worth it. Not to us. We won't blow our deal with the Houses over some Touched who owes you money."

"The Houses won't find out this came from you," Amar insists.

"I don't care," Blue retorts. "If they did—"

"It's not about money."

I blink when I realize I've blurted the words out. I can't worry about it, though. These people can help find Ruby. There's something going on that *kills* Touched people, and these two can help me save her from that. But they're not, because of Amar's lies.

To hell with his orders, then.

The girl studies me, her gaze guarded.

"It's about my friend," I persist. "Volgert took her because they think I'm with House Linden, even though

I'm not. But if I don't get her back soon—" I swallow hard. "Please just tell us where to find her."

I don't even breathe. I can't believe I'm begging for sympathy from a vampire.

Leaf looks back at Blue. Her pale eyes meet his, considering and wary at the same time.

"We don't know where they're keeping them," she admits.

My heart sinks. I want to cry.

"But we do know where they're going to be," Blue continues. "Terchett Wharf. The abandoned fishery there." She glances at Amar. "Set starts tonight at sundown."

Amar looks away like he's swearing inside.

"They won't bring in the Touched till shortly before that, though," Blue says before I can ask. "Houses always hide their stock—they don't want anyone messing with them before a set—but Volgert especially is going above and beyond this time. They're running this one, and they almost didn't even invite *us* in, they were so hung up on secrecy."

Her eyes flick to me, and my stomach rolls when I read between the lines. It's because of me. Linden too, perhaps, but also me.

For all Kyle's talk, they don't want anyone going after Ruby.

Air leaves me. I can't decide whether to be grateful or terrified at the information, and the weirdly pitying look on the girl's face isn't helping. She's a *vampire*, for God's sake.

And I'm a succubus. And apparently nothing is like what I've read in storybooks.

My heart won't stop racing. I have so many questions, I feel like I'm going to explode.

Amar doesn't give me a chance to ask. He pushes to his feet and extends a hand, pulling me up after him. Dropping my hand immediately once I reach my feet, he heads for the door. "Thanks," he says to the vampires.

"That was bullshit, you know," Blue replies. "You lying to us like that."

He doesn't say anything, and after a moment, her mouth tightens like she gets his reasoning anyway. Leaf pulls open the door. For the first time, I notice how careful he is to stay within the entryway's shadows.

I'm not sure what to do. I follow Amar toward the exit, only to glance back when I reach it.

Blue is still watching me.

"Thank you," I tell her.

She nods. I glance at Leaf, including him in the statement.

He shrugs. "You see us tonight, you don't know us, okay?"

"Okay," I agree nervously.

I trail Amar out into the sunlight. Around us, the rushing of the water and bird calls are the only sounds. The sun's climbed higher since we went inside, the pink-gold tones of early morning vanishing into ordinary daylight. The dock is nearly deserted despite the hour, however. I only see one other person: a bald man in a leather jacket, smoking a cigarette while he leans against the flood wall.

And he's watching us.

I freeze. He's several dozen yards away, but I swear he's looking right at me. The attention sends shivers running down my spine.

"Amar," I say, throwing a glance at him. "Who is—"

The man is gone when I turn back.

I stare, a rough breath leaving me. He was there. A big guy, all alone in the bright sunlight.

"Come on."

I look at Amar. "There was a—"

"I know." He strides down the walkway like nothing happened.

"Well, do you know who it was?"

He's silent for a heartbeat. "No."

I hesitate, my eyes twitching toward the flood wall again. This can't be good. I mean…

Amar is almost to the car.

I hurry after him. "Okay. Then, um… what now?"

He doesn't look my way. I can't tell if he's mad at me, them, or the information we've been given—or even if he's mad at all. Expressionless, he continues toward the sedan. I jog after him.

"Amar?"

He tugs open the door. "Now we find Ruby before sunset."

19

RUBY

She's huddling in the corner of the cage, and no matter how she tries, she can't stop shaking. Her whole body trembles. Her fingers claw nervously at her legs when she's not focused on them, like they're no longer under her control.

Kyle's gone. The big guy too, though he's come back a few times. It's harder now, being scared of that one. She knows she should be. Knows it's important to remember to be afraid of the large man with the scars. New fears have taken over, though. They make it hard to concentrate.

He gave her something, that man. Gives her something every time he stops at the cage. His hand clamps on her ankle, and early on, she'd tried to scream.

She has trouble remembering why she'd screamed.

Pleasure had rolled through her at his touch, the sensation hot and sparkling like that time in Billy Cormack's basement when his parents were away. It surged through her body, building stronger and stronger, shredding her thoughts and leaving her mind in tatters in its wake.

Her fingers scratch at her jeans. She closes her eyes, strug-

gling to still them, struggling to focus on the cold cage and the frigid floor and all the sensations that ground her against the one that comes when the big man puts his hand on her.

Footsteps sound on the concrete. Her concentration shatters. Her heart climbs her throat, and her eyes lock on the door.

The large man steps into view. Her hands twitch out of her control.

"Come," he orders.

She bites her lip, resisting the impulse to move toward him. She tastes blood.

The door opens. He reaches in. Her leg spasms, flinching toward him, and his lips pull back in a yellow-toothed smile.

And then his meaty palm lands on her ankle.

The world goes blurry. Heat spreads between her legs, and moisture too, and distantly, she feels her body sag against the cage wall. The pleasure rolls through her, taking the cold of the steel bars away. Sweat breaks out over her skin, and she moans with the waves coursing through her body. Her legs fall toward him, spreading wide. She's terrified he'll stop. She'll do anything for him if he'll just not stop.

He drags her closer. Her body flops to the floor. She can't control it. Doesn't care. The grit of the rough ground scrapes her skin while he hauls her across the cage, and then his hand is on her face.

Her eyes widen. The world flashes white. This is better than Billy. Better than anything in the world. She's wet now, so wet, and her body is paralyzed by pleasure. She has to know what he wants from her. What she can do for him so he'll stay. She stares up at him, begging him with her eyes to tell her, and he grins at the sight.

He takes his hand away.

A shriek leaves her. She scrambles up from the floor, her body aching like her blood has been turned to stone.

He slams the door. She shoves an arm through the bars, grasping after him, pleading for him to come back in wild noises that she doesn't recognize. Sensations are returning—the cold of the steel cage, the ice of the floor—and she hates them. She wants his touch again. She wants to know what will make him bring that feeling back.

Because fighting isn't important anymore. Nothing is. She has to get that feeling back again.

It's the only thing that matters in the world.

IF SILENCE WAS A MARTIAL ART, AMAR WOULD BE A MASTER.

"So where do you think they'll have her?" I ask.

No response. I watch him steer the car around a minivan.

"Do you know anyone who can get us past Volgert's security?"

He turns the sedan around a corner. The parking garage of Bianca's building comes into view.

My heart pounds. I feel like a child pestering the big grown-up with questions.

I feel like shrieking at him for treating me that way.

"Amar, what's a set?"

His jaw muscles jump. He steers the sedan into a parking space and then gets out of the car without a word.

I stare after him, flabbergasted. I want to grab him and shake him for his damnable silence.

But like so much else, I know it wouldn't do any good.

I climb from the car. Screw this. Maybe shaking him won't work, but I'll still find a way to get that man to talk to me—and *before* we end up in Bianca's apartment and I have to deal with her again.

He's already reached the elevator. I stride after him. "Amar, goddammit, you can't just—"

My cell rings.

I falter, flustered by the sound, and for a moment, I have the irrational fear it'll be Kyle. Or Ruby, screaming and insane. Or hell, maybe just my stepmom. I fumble the phone from my pocket and then stare, not recognizing the number.

I look back toward the elevator. Amar is watching me. The doors have opened, and he hasn't made a move to go past them.

I answer the call. "Hello?"

"Is this Caitlin Faire?" The man's voice is cold. Businesslike.

I hesitate. "Who's this?"

"Am I speaking to Caitlin Faire?" he persists, his tone hardening.

"Uh, yeah?" I manage, watching as Amar strides back toward me.

"Miss Faire, my name is Lieutenant Reyes of the Corvinson Police. I'm calling in regard to your apartment. There's been a break-in. I'm going to have to ask you to come to the police station to help us with this situation."

I look at Amar as he comes up beside me.

"Who is it?" he mouths.

I cover the receiver. "Police," I whisper back.

He grimaces.

"Miss Faire?"

I uncover the phone quickly. "Uh, sorry. Um…"

"Are you all right, Miss Faire?" The cop's voice has an edge to it now.

"Yeah. Yeah, sorry. A break-in?"

"I can have an officer pick you up, but we're going to need—"

"No," I say hurriedly. "I mean…" I look at Amar. He jerks his chin at Bianca's sedan. I let out a ragged breath and nod. "I'll be there in a few minutes."

"Very well. One more question, though, Miss Faire. We haven't been able to reach your roommate. Is she with you?"

I tremble. "I-I haven't seen her."

The cop pauses. "Very well. Come to the front desk and ask for me. Lieutenant Reyes."

"Okay."

I hang up.

Amar doesn't give me a chance to ask him any questions. Taking out his phone, he thumbs it on and then lifts it to his ear.

"Cops called her," he says shortly. My brow furrows. "Yeah, we're going there now. Yeah. Sundown, today. Terchett Wharf. Thank you."

He lowers the phone. "Come on," he continues to me, his tone unchanged. "Bianca will look into things while we're gone."

Without another word, he heads for the car.

⌘

I don't get anything out of Amar while we drive to the station, and after a few minutes, I give up. This is ridiculous. Infuriating, rude, childish, and ridiculous.

And it's beginning to scare the hell out of me.

I lock my gaze on the window while the city rolls by. Amar's been close-mouthed before. Hell, the guy probably has a patent on that, and normally, it's plenty enough to drive me insane. But this…

This has to be bad. Like, epic bad. The more I think about it, the clearer that becomes. He told me we were demons. He told me about his mom and his sadistic dad. He's not exactly chatty, but barriers had been dropping between us, even if only a little bit.

And now they're back.

On steroids.

And that's terrifying.

Amar pulls the car to a stop outside the station, and when I glance at him, I swear I catch a flicker of discomfort on his face. The walls are cracking. Maybe, anyway.

But then he shoves open the door and leaves the car, and by the time I get out of the sedan, the ice is back tenfold.

I want to be mad at it. I want to summon up the energy to scream at him for shutting me out like this, for knowing what's going on and not telling me, for pulling away all the time.

Because anger distracts me from fear, and right now, I just want to stop trembling.

"If they ask," he says when we reach the door, "we were together last night at my apartment, okay?"

I nod. He echoes the motion and then heads through the entrance. I follow.

The urge to run hits me the moment we set foot inside.

A desk waits ahead, guarded by a panel of sliding glass and featuring a woman behind it who looks like the world could end and she wouldn't blink. Butterscotch walls surround us while panel lights in the drop ceiling do their damnedest to glare on the scuffed linoleum below. In the chairs against the wall to our left, I see a random assortment of people already here despite the relatively early hour.

Several of them stare at us, their eyes tracking our every movement while we cross the room to the desk.

"Um, excuse me?" I try when we reach the window.

The woman glances up.

"Lieutenant Reyes called me. Asked me to come in?"

The woman could give Amar a run for his money on the ice thing. "And your name?"

"Sorry. Caitlin Faire."

I can't read anything from her expression. She picks up the phone and punches a few numbers. "Caitlin Faire to see you." She pauses. "Yes, sir."

The woman returns the phone to its cradle. "He'll be with you in a moment. Please have a seat." She motions to the chairs by the wall. We cross the room and sit down on the cold plastic.

Minutes creep along, gathering one after the other like slow torture. By my side, Amar is silent. He might as well be a stranger.

I swallow hard, pushing the thought aside.

A door on the far end of the room opens. "Miss Faire?"

I blink and look up. A stocky man is walking toward us. He's got a bearing like a hammer, all blunt force and hard, and his dark hair has been shaved so short, he looks bald.

With Amar, I rise to my feet. I take the man's hand when he extends it.

"Lieutenant Reyes," he says. "Thank you for coming in."

I give a vague approximation of a nod. "Have you heard anything from Ruby?"

Lieutenant Reyes pauses. "Not as yet." He glances from

me to Amar and then motions back the way he came. "If you'd join me…?"

My head bobbles again. We follow him past the door and into a windowless room arrayed with blocky desks. Other cops are there; they don't look up when we pass.

"My apologies for the delay in alerting you to the break-in," the lieutenant says while we walk. "We were only able to retrieve your phone number from your land-lord this morning."

"That's okay," I manage.

He stops at a wooden rectangle of a desk. The top is taken up by a flat monitor, a keyboard, and enough in-trays and out-trays to make a secretary weep. Manila folders reside in both, stacked one atop the other with cryptic codes on their flaps. Two metal chairs are stationed nearby. We sit down, Amar looking infinitely more calm than I do.

But then he's good at that sort of thing.

"Now," the lieutenant continues, taking a seat and then selecting a pencil from a jar near his keyboard. He brings out a small notebook from inside his pocket and flips it open. "Miss Faire, about your roommate."

My hands tangle with each other and clench down hard.

"Do you have any idea where we might find her?"

I shake my head. I can't take my eyes off him. "No."

"Do you have any reason to suspect her absence is related to the break-in? An angry ex-boyfriend, perhaps? Or difficulty with a coworker?"

My fingers tighten. My knuckles are probably going white. "No."

He looks down. His pencil scratches on the notebook.

My eyes lock on the paper. I wonder what he's writing

down. "D-do you think something's happened to her?" I work to keep my voice from giving anything away.

Lieutenant Reyes's dark gaze flicks up to me. "We want to make sure that's not the case."

I force myself to nod. Smile, albeit nervously.

He finishes writing. "Where were you last night, Miss Faire?"

"I—" My head twitches toward Amar. "I was at his place."

Lieutenant Reyes's focus goes to Amar and then back to me. I can't tell what he thinks of the statement. "What time did you leave your apartment?"

"Um, nine, maybe? I-I didn't really check the clock." I shrug.

"Was your roommate there when you—"

"Sir?" comes a woman's voice.

Lieutenant Reyes looks beyond me. I turn.

And freeze.

"Ah, Cait." Alistair Linden walks toward us, ignoring the receptionist when she slips back toward her desk. "How fortunate to find you here."

I stare at the short gray-haired man in his expensive suit and at the pair of enormous henchmen beside him. Both of them tower over the old man like something from a cartoon. There's a skinny rail of a guy several steps behind them, his entire body narrow and stretched like reality is tighter in his world.

I can't decide what to do. Some irrational part of me still wants to blurt out that I need House Linden's help. To agree to anything, if only he'll save Ruby.

But the rest of me…

Shivers pool in my middle, growing colder and more agitated by the second. Alistair's got this smooth smile on his lips. There's a look in his eyes like everything from the cops to the drywall exists only at his whim.

And all I'm reminded of is Kyle. His arrogance. His contempt. When the old man had his henchmen bring me to his restaurant, he'd assured me he wasn't an incubus.

But every instinct I have screams he might as well be.

Alistair turns his pleasant smile on the cop. "Lieutenant Reyes, isn't it? Hello. I'm here on behalf of the young lady." He motions to the skinny man behind him, who steps forward as if summoned. "Mister Finley, my attorney."

"She's not under arrest," Lieutenant Reyes retorts incredulously.

"Consider it a precaution."

"Cait doesn't need your assistance, Mister Linden," Amar says. "We've already established she wasn't involved in this."

"Truly?" Alistair regards us both questioningly. "And how exactly have you established that?"

Amar is silent.

"Miss Faire says she was with this gentleman at his home last night," Lieutenant Reyes fills in slowly, like he's testing the statement and everyone's reactions alike.

Humor flickers over Alistair's face. "At your home, Mister Okoro. The two of you."

It's not quite a question. It almost sounds like he's telling a joke. "Yeah," I reply.

The old man transforms the amusement into a smile. "But of course. How nice to hear you're dating." He looks to the lieutenant. "Now, unless you have some pertinent questions for the young lady, I believe she's been bothered enough. Her apartment was ransacked. Surely, that's sufficient stress for one day."

For a moment, the cop doesn't say anything. His eyes narrow slightly, like he's reading something into the words, and then his focus twitches to the lawyer. Behind his tiny, metal-rimmed glasses, Mister Finley regards the lieutenant with eyes like a dead fish.

"We'll be in touch," Lieutenant Reyes says to me.

"I'm certain Mister Finley will be happy to arrange any conversations you might require," Alistair fills in before I can speak.

The lieutenant pauses again, and then he draws a business card from his pocket. He slides it across the desk to me. "If you think of anything, call me."

I take the card and nod quickly. The chairs scrape on the floor when Amar and I rise.

Alistair smiles. "Pleasure to meet you, Lieutenant."

Reyes nods once but doesn't say anything.

Alistair's expression doesn't change. With a wave of his hand, he motions for Amar and me to precede him toward the station door.

"After you," Amar counters, nothing in his tone. No sarcasm, no fear. He could be commenting on the weather.

Alistair's smile broadens. With his henchmen and his lawyer around him, he heads for the exit.

I look at Amar. He glances toward me, displeasure with the situation flickering through his eyes, and then he leads the way after them.

"So," Alistair says when we reach the concrete stairway outside. "*That* was fascinating."

I try to ignore him, scanning the area around us for more threats. The morning sunlight has turned to a glare, reflecting from the sandstone walls and casting short little stubs of shadows from the towering oak trees on the lawn surrounding the station. Cars slip by on the road, moving with a slowness that makes it clear they're studiously obeying the speed limit till they get some distance from where all the cops stay.

But I don't see anyone else. No demons—not that I could tell them from humans anyway. But there's nobody at all.

"Why are you here?" Amar demands.

"Now, Mister Okoro, no need to be rude. Some of my people informed me that the lieutenant had contacted Cait. I wanted to make sure nothing untoward happened."

I resist the urge to retreat from Alistair, possibly into the next county. The only way "his people" would have known about Lieutenant Reyes calling me is if they're at the station too. Or tapping my phone.

Neither is a comforting possibility. Meanwhile, he's still smiling in this kindly way that nevertheless reminds me of a jackal. "Why are you so interested in me?" I ask.

Alistair makes a surprised and confused noise. "My dear, why wouldn't I be interested in helping someone new to our world?"

I bite back a scoff. The words are bullshit. They have to be, said like that, with enough saccharin innocence to make teeth rot. They absolutely have to be.

"Is this about Kyle?" I press.

His brow rises innocently. "Who?"

I don't know what to say. What won't endanger me, or Ruby. Maybe even Amar. "A guy who keeps following me around. The 'Volgert lackey' your people saw the other day." I hesitate. "He said they're coming after your House again."

Alistair makes a noise of understanding. "Ah, yes. That." He smiles. "Well, never fear. The damage to the Protected was most unfortunate, to be sure, but it was a minor oversight. We now have the situation *thoroughly* under control."

I eye him, my skin crawling for no reason I can pinpoint. There's something more to the words, though, like the threat against his people has become almost a joke.

"As for why I am, as you say, *interested* in you..." The old man sighs indulgently. "My dear, it's simple enough. You're in trouble. When someone is in trouble, only a monster would refuse to provide assistance. And we're not that, so why shouldn't we reach out to you?"

Amar puts a hand to my back like he's had enough.

"Come on," he says, attempting to lead me around Alistair's bodyguards.

"Cait," Alistair persists. "I'd be careful if I were you. You're competition to your kind. One more hungry mouth on the hunting grounds. They won't *really* help you, no matter what they might claim."

I don't look at Amar. I don't look at anyone. Locking my eyes on the concrete steps, I hurry down to the sidewalk.

"Your friend stands very little chance of surviving tonight," Alistair calls. "The pit match that I hear they have planned for her…" He makes a tutting noise.

I stop. Amar's hand presses my back. I ignore the silent entreaty to keep moving and look back at Alistair. "What?"

Alistair's brow rises. He descends the steps toward where I stand rooted to the sidewalk like my feet have become one with the concrete. "You didn't know that? The set, my dear, where the Touched are made to attack one another like dogs in fights to the death. Sets are big business for some of the Houses. They bring in sizable crowds, money from bets on who will win, and all manner of advantages to those who deem such profits worthy of human blood. Murderers and rapists who've been turned into Touched typically fill the ranks, as well as the occasional innocent." He gives me a helplessly apologetic look. "And now, of course, your friend is there as well."

I can't even move. The words just ring in my head, awkward and utterly wrong. From the corner of my eye, I can see Amar looking at me.

"I mean, it's *possible* your friend might survive tonight," Alistair allows. "Volgert must have high hopes for her, fast-tracking her into a set so quickly. Though honestly, only the most vicious last beyond—"

"Enough," Amar snaps. "Where is Volgert keeping her?"

The old man scoffs. "Oh, please, Mister Okoro. I don't simply have those sorts of details at hand. My people know the most widely spread information. A rumor here or there, but—"

"So how do you know about her?" I ask.

Alistair pauses. "Well," he amends. "We *do* have informants inside Volgert. That's how I heard about your friend, and how I knew what danger she was in. Perhaps if you'd taken me up on the offer earlier…" He shrugs.

I stare at him. As manipulation goes, this is as subtle as a brick.

That doesn't mean it's not working.

I can't look at Amar. He knew this. From the moment those vampires said the set was tonight—hell, even before that—he knew what was going to happen to Ruby.

And he never told me. He insisted that I go to sleep. That I stay at Bianca's. That I come here, to some goddamn police station, when my best friend was going to be thrown into a dog fight to the *death* in only a few *hours*.

My whole world is shaking. I can't make it stop. I suspected Amar was hiding something, but… but *this*?

"Mister Linden." I hardly recognize the sound of my own voice. It's too calm. Too normal, when really I should be screaming. "About that offer."

His eyebrow lifts like he doesn't have a clue what I could be asking. Like he's just politely curious. Deep inside my gut, a coil of hatred twists hot and venomous for the expression, but I don't let that stop me from continuing. "What can you do to save my friend?"

"Cait," Amar protests.

I don't turn toward him. "If you don't know where she is, then what guarantee do I have that you can—"

Amar snags my arm. I yank myself from his grasp, not taking my eyes from the old man.

But the shaking gets worse. Colder, like everything is freezing inside me. Like I might shatter at any moment. I'm agreeing to murder. To *being* a murderer.

And leaving my friend to die tonight isn't the same thing?

"My dear," Alistair says, "I could order my informants to work on finding her whereabouts immediately. I have no doubt I could locate her before the set begins. It's risky, though. Volgert isn't fond of us, as I'm sure you're aware. I'd only undertake something that perilous for a member of my House. Though if that's what you're proposing…?"

Amar steps between us. "Don't *do* this, Cait. You need to—"

"That's what I'm proposing," I agree, raising my voice over Amar's words. I try to move past him. "I'm saying that I'll—"

Amar grabs me and propels me backward so quickly, my words die in a strangled gasp. The sunlight falls behind the leaves of a tree, and then the world disappears. Darkness and gray mist whip around me. The ground lurches beneath my feet.

Light returns, and then my back slams into a wall. The air leaves my lungs in a rush. Amar is still holding onto me. I choke and shove at him. He moves back fast.

I gasp for a breath, my chest burning from the sudden evacuation of oxygen. We're on a large balcony, but it's not Bianca's. The space around me is a lengthy rectangle, walled on two sides and open to the world on the others. It's stark, though. Gray and bare, with only a sliding door of reflective glass as a feature. A metal railing runs around the space, as plain as the rest of it. We're at least ten stories up. The morning sunlight ends only inches from my sandals.

My eyes return to where Amar leans on the patio rail, his breathing hard and fast like his heart is racing.

"What the *hell*?" I demand.

"You were making a mistake."

My brow climbs. The burning in my lungs is fading.

But the ice-cold trembling that's gripped me for hours on end isn't going anywhere. "You bastard, you don't get to decide what's a—"

"You can't join House Linden, Cait. Not like this."

I don't even know what to say.

His jaw muscles jump. "You need to—"

"No! Just… no." My head shakes. "You son of a bitch…"

I shove away from the wall and stride past him, heading for the patio door. I have no idea where I am. I don't care.

Oh my God, he *knew* about this.

"Dammit." Amar grabs my arm. "You don't—"

Static surges over me, hot and weird, and his grip vanishes. A pained noise follows. I look back fast.

He's on his knees by the railing, one hand bracing him against the concrete patio floor. His chest is heaving for air, and his body shakes like he's been electrically shocked.

For a moment, I stare. I did that. I hurt him.

I can't figure out if I wanted to.

Tears sting my eyes. "You didn't tell me. You *knew*, and you just—"

"You think I wanted to tell you that?" His gaze snaps to

mine, furious and pained. "You think for one goddamn *second* that I wanted to tell you—"

"Why do you even *care?* You bastard..." My face crumples while I fight back a sob. "Why do you—"

"Because I don't want this to hurt you!"

I tremble.

He pushes to his feet. I tense, retreating.

Amar pauses at the sight. "I was going to take care of it," he continues, his calm tone forced. "Bianca, Brett, all of us. We'd fix this, we'd get Ruby back, and you'd never..." He seems to struggle with how to finish the sentence.

But I can guess what he'd intended to say. I'd never have known. About the death matches, about the hell Ruby must be going through. The one I can't save her from, not on my own. Not without selling my body and soul to a psychopath.

My arms wrap around my middle, trying to stop my shivering.

"I didn't want you to see this, Cait," Amar says softly. "How fucked up this world is. That was never the plan."

My voice is shaky when I speak. "What was?"

"Show you only what you need to know. Enough to keep you safe. And then just... just let you..."

Amar shakes his head, a strange mix of regret and frustration on his face, like words keep tripping him up, and he can't figure out why. And the look doesn't change anything. It doesn't make the hurt of this nightmare disappear.

But some of my rage at him drains anyway.

"I'm sorry," he continues. "I wasn't trying to—" He grimaces, giving up. "I'm sorry."

"Why do you care?" I whisper.

His gaze drops to the floor for a moment, his brow

furrowing like he's lost somehow. Then his eyes lift again. They turn to the view beyond the balcony, to the world out there, something so hard in his expression.

In silence, he walks to the patio door. I watch him, confused. He pulls the reflective glass aside and then twitches his head toward the space beyond it, motioning for me to go ahead of him.

My arms still hugging my stomach, I step past him. An apartment as stark as the balcony meets my eyes. Dove-gray walls with white trim surround stiff furniture that doesn't look designed for humans to sit upon. A glossy black television hangs above a fireplace while, beyond the living room, there's a kitchen with marble counters, steel appliances, and a breakfast bar. A hallway extends off to my left, lost in shadows, and ahead of me lies the white front door.

And that's it. The place is as crisp and cold as a magazine photo. There's no art. No decorations. Not a single personal touch at all.

"Where are we?" I ask.

Amar slides the door shut behind us. "My apartment."

I look back. He pauses by the door as if weighing what to do, and then he comes toward me. I tense, but don't move away. He stops in front of me. My eyes skirt around. I want to look at him, but I still feel so raw that I'm shaking.

"I need you safe, all right?" he says softly. "That's the reason for all of this. For the people I've hired. For the way *they're* the ones tearing this city apart right now, not you. Volgert and the people who've taken Ruby… This is only the barest edge of what they're capable of doing. I can't let that happen. Not to you."

"But… why? Why do you care if I'm—"

"Because you're innocent."

My gaze inches toward his. "Innocent?"

He hesitates. "Human."

I can't figure out what to say. The demons… they hate that. Emotion. Humanity. And Amar pulls away from me so often, half the time I'm not sure he doesn't feel the same.

"I don't want you to lose that," he continues. "I don't want you to have to…"

Grimacing, he trails off, but it almost doesn't matter. I can read what he would have said on his face.

To have to become like him.

My chest aches in spite of everything, and I'm not sure why. Whether I'm hurting for him and what he thinks he is, or for my fear of what he might be. Of all the things about him I don't know.

"It's dangerous, though," he continues. "For you…" His hand takes mine, and gently, he eases my fingers away from where they grip my elbow. "For me."

The confused mess of my emotions grows.

He watches our hands in that way he has: distant, meditative. "They use anything you care about. Anything can become a vulnerability. And—" His mouth tightens briefly. "And if they knew about the way I've started to feel around you… the way I can't stop thinking about you, they'd…"

I look away fast, my chest quivering harder. My eyes land on the apartment. On the cold walls and the stiff furniture.

On the utter lack of a single thing to lose.

His hand comes up, brushing my face, pulling my attention back to him. "I don't want you to disappear."

He's so close now. So warm. My thoughts are scattered.

Frayed and raw and painful to touch. I can't understand them.

His presence is turning them to an aching mush.

Carefully, his fingers slip into my hair. I'm trembling, something inside me yearning to bridge the distance between us. To draw closer, where I could feel his warmth wrapping all around me.

But I should be looking for Ruby. I *should*. My best friend could die tonight. She could be thrown into a pit and made to fight for her life. And the only thing I can do to stop it is offer myself up to a psycho.

Or trust Amar.

A strange stillness settles over me. That's it, isn't it? The alternative—the only one. I could trust him. Trust this man who hid this horrible secret, but only to protect me. Trust this man who's helped me over and over again, even if he hardly knows me.

Though, really, that last part isn't true. In only a few short days, he knows more about me than anyone but Ruby.

And he's still here.

"We'll find her," he whispers to me. "I *swear* to you, we will find her."

I nod, unable to meet his gaze. From the corner of my eye, I see him echo the motion, but otherwise, he's still.

And then a small breath escapes him. He starts to move away.

"No," I gasp softly.

He stops.

Blood throbs in my veins. I'm so raw. So cold.

And yet…

Tremulously, my hand rises, finding his side, feeling his muscles through his shirt. I hear his breath catch. I inch nearer, surrounding myself with his scent, his warmth.

With the way he makes me feel safe.

He hesitates and then bends slightly. His face is close to mine, just beyond touch, just at the edge of brushing my skin, and he whispers, "Do you want me to?"

I nod again. "Yes."

He turns then, and his lips take mine. Heat spreads through me, washing away fear and doubt and all of the world beyond the feeling of him here. My hand tightens on him, drawing him closer. I'd missed this. Needed this.

Because just for a moment, it makes this nightmare go away.

He pulls me to him, pressing my body to his. The kiss deepens, his tongue twisting against me, his mouth devouring mine. I can feel him through my jeans, growing hard for me.

Hot desire floods my veins.

In a swift motion, his hands slip around my sides and he lifts me. I gasp, and on instinct, I wrap my legs around him to brace myself. His hardness presses on my crotch, and unexpected pleasure bubbles up through me, shocking and yet unbelievably welcome. My legs tighten on him, bringing him closer, and against my lips, he makes a hungry noise.

Shifting his grip, he grabs my ass with one hand while the other rakes up through my hair, pinning my mouth to his. He moves then, carrying me with him, never taking his lips from mine. I can't believe he's navigating through the apartment blind.

I wonder how many times he's done this.

The thought is a splinter, and I yank it away fast. I don't want to think about that right now, about anything.

Anything except him.

We pass through the hall. I can feel the air shift around us when he turns, and my eyelids crack open. We're in a bedroom. Gray walls surround us, trimmed with white like the living room. Twilight dimness pervades the space, lightened only by the faint sunlight passing through windows draped with long gray curtains. A four-post bed takes up much of one wall while a black dresser and night-stands make up the rest of the furniture.

He reaches the bedside, and bracing himself with one knee on the mattress, he lowers me down. My back sinks onto the silken comforter, and my head rests on thick pillows. The scent of lavender and detergent puffs up around me. I barely notice. My eyes are locked on Amar.

His lips rise in that secretive, promising smile that he does so well. The one that sends a thrill running through my veins every time I see it. And now is no different. The flesh between my legs burns hotter at the sight. His smile is all I can see.

He retreats from the bed and straightens at the side of it. Smoothly, he pulls his shirt over his head and returns his gaze to mine like he doesn't want to lose sight of me even for a moment. My lips part. I can't help it. My eyes devour his dark, gorgeous skin pulled taut across the muscles of his arms and torso.

His smile broadens. He unfastens his jeans and slides them down.

Adrenaline rushes through me, pebbling my skin, making my breasts tingle. I can't believe this is happening. His erection strains at the fabric of his black briefs, and the sight leaves me simultaneously shy and entranced.

He moves toward me again. I'm barely breathing. The world feels like it's moving too fast and too slow all at the same time. Gently, he takes my feet and slides my sandals away. One after the other, they thud to the floor. He smiles again, and then rises a bit, drawing closer to me. Carefully, he takes the lowest button of my blouse. His fingers brush the skin of my abdomen. I stop breathing entirely. Moisture is spreading between my legs, hot and unstoppable. I'm throbbing for him.

Slowly, he works his way up the pink blouse, his gaze on mine. The temperature of the air on my skin drops as the two sides of the shirt lose contact with each other, baring my stomach. I bite my lip. He pauses, almost in reaction to the simple motion, and something turns dark and hungry in his eyes.

Pink fabric falls aside, exposing my cheap strapless bra to the cool air. I wish I'd worn something fancier. I wish I *owned* something fancier.

The thought doesn't last long. His hands move for the closure of my borrowed jeans, and my insides twist tighter at the feeling of him there. The zipper releases. His fingers slide beneath the waistband, teasing along skin no one else has ever touched with such care as this.

With agonizing slowness, he eases the jeans away from me, and my panties go with them. I hear the jeans hit the floor, hear the bedsprings give when he climbs onto the mattress. But I can't take my eyes from him. It's like the whole room has faded away.

His hands slide up behind me, and I arch my back quickly. My heart is pounding, ricocheting against my ribs as if it's broken free of its moorings to bounce out of control. My bra loosens. He pulls it aside. I'm naked before him.

I wonder what he thinks of what he sees.

Amar's smile returns, a look in his eyes like he can

practically read what I'm thinking. "God, you're beautiful," he whispers.

The burning inside me gets worse. Stronger.

An awe-filled look drifts over his face. "So beautiful."

I can't breathe.

He turns his gaze to my body then, to the path of his hand ghosting over my midsection, moving lower. A stilted breath leaves me, a question lost somewhere in the airy sound.

Amar glances back, this incredible confidence in his eyes. He knows exactly what he's doing. "I want to give you this first. Is that all right?"

My brow twitches lower, but I nod. His fingers slip between my legs, down to the wet skin there. I gasp. On instinct, my hips lift toward his hand, hungry for more of his touch, and Amar gives a soft laugh.

The sound is incredible.

Gently, his fingertip plays across my clit, and I lose the ability to breathe all over again. My insides twist and my body tenses, caught up in the surges of pleasure that flare through me while he rubs and explores every bit of the sensitive skin. He teases me a moment longer before his touch slides lower. Slides inside me.

My eyes widen.

Amar makes a satisfied noise like he enjoys what he's feeling. He curls his finger then, stroking me from the inside. The sensation is unbelievable. I twitch at the feeling of it, unable to stop myself. His other hand rises to my breast, cupping it in his palm, closing in till he reaches my nipple. He pinches his fingers around it. A jolt of pleasure shoots through me.

His smile doesn't fade. Bending over me, he lowers his

mouth toward my breast, his eyes on mine. His tongue slips across the hardened nub, twisting around it.

My body flinches in response, a stronger spike of pleasure rocketing through me, and I gasp again. He doesn't stop, his hand continuing its motion inside me while his mouth plays across skin that has become so much more sensitive than I ever realized it could be. I feel like I'm being set on fire. Like my body has been transformed into an instrument, one Amar knows how to play impossibly well. Tingling sensations begin to rush through my veins, hot and bubbling and centered around his amazing hands. I writhe under him while he continues onward, stroking me, nipping at my breasts and neck, laying kisses and feather-light touches all across my flesh.

The fire grows higher. Hotter. My breaths are ragged. Sweat breaks out over my skin. I rock beneath his touch while an urgency builds inside me—this desperate feeling like, if he doesn't continue, I don't know what I'll do. I want this. I *need* this. He's scarcely even *inside* me yet, nothing more than his finger anyway, but he already feels so good that I—

The feeling explodes, rushing through my body all the way down to my toes. A cry rips from me. My fingers clench on the bedspread, hanging on for dear life even while my hips push at his hand, instinctively trying to wring every ounce of pleasure out of this I can get.

And gradually, the crescendo fades. I can barely think. I'm gasping for breath, my mind in awe of what just ripped it to shreds.

Amar's hand leaves my breast. His other hand slips from inside me. I open my eyes to find him watching me.

Improbable shyness flutters up out of nowhere. I worry

what I looked like. What he thought. What it felt like for him, touching me.

But he simply smiles. "Good?"

My brow climbs. Good? Is he *nuts*? Good doesn't even come *near* that feeling.

I nod. "Uh-huh."

"Do you want to keep going?"

I stare at him. I can only think of one response. "Oh my God, yes."

2 2

I THINK AMAR'S SMILE MIGHT BE THE MOST BEAUTIFUL THING I've ever seen.

Chuckling, he leans away from me, reaching toward the black nightstand. He tugs open the drawer and retrieves a foil-wrapped packet from inside.

I bite my lip. I know what I said.

That doesn't mean I'm actually *ready* for this, though.

He shifts around and then pauses, his gaze flicking back to mine. Watching me, he pulls his briefs away.

Shivers run over my skin at the sight of him. His dark cock looks all the larger now for not having any cloth covering him. It's intimidating, really. But so amazing that the skin between my legs starts to throb all over again.

The corner of his mouth rises in another smile. He rips the packet open, takes the condom out, rolls it on easily. My throat closes, nervousness choking me. He moves like he's done this a thousand times.

He probably has.

I bash the thought down. My God, I don't need that

right now. Not with him there, huge and ready and hotter than the surface of the sun. He comes back toward me. I quiver, anxious as hell and yet aching with anticipation.

Gently, he moves my legs apart. His fingers stray over me again, playing across the insides of my thighs. My breath catches. He comes closer. His cock brushes my sensitive lips down there, and it's like every inch of my body goes on alert. All of my attention suddenly locks on that tiny sensation, the tip of him moving against me, getting wet with my moisture. And I'm scared. It hurts, I know. What comes next. I don't even breathe, waiting for the pain to begin.

But Amar pauses. He watches me for a moment, and then he bends over me till he reaches my earlobe, and his tongue plays along its edge. My focus scatters, suddenly torn between the sensations of him touching me and the warmth of his body right above mine. The smell of him fills my head, spicy but musky and so incredibly arousing. His left arm braces him on the mattress while his other hand moves down, parting the folds between my legs, rubbing over my clit in intense little circles that make tingles of pleasure run wild through my veins.

And then he starts to enter me.

I gasp and then wince. It hurts. It really does hurt. A sharp, pinching pain that doesn't feel natural. That makes some part of my brain instantly argue that something is horribly wrong. He slides in deeper, and I bite down on my lip hard, fighting not to make a sound that'll worry him. I don't want him to stop. Not really. I don't think so, anyway. Maybe. I mean, I know he will if I ask him to, but unless something really *is*—

He stops moving. My eyes dart around, uncertain, but then he starts again. Gentle. Slow. Easing out a bit and then back in, over and over, going deeper every time. I feel so strange. So full and strange.

And good.

I don't know when it happens. One moment, I'm intensely conscious of the pain, and the next, I realize it's somehow stepped aside, and the most amazing feeling—the most natural feeling in the world—is taking its place. My body begins to move with his, rocking carefully against the silken surface of the comforter, and my whole being is caught up in the feel of him. He's so deep inside me, his body sending hot and wonderful pulses through my clit with every powerful thrust. I listen to instinct before shyness can catch me, and I reach up, my hands clutching his ass, pulling him against me as tightly as I can.

He groans, the sound thick and heavy with desire. A thrill shoots through me at the noise, at the feeling of his strong muscles flexing beneath my grip. Holy crap, I'm having sex with him. With Amar. I mean, duh, but oh my *God*, I—

A new feeling spreads up through me, hot and shivery and a million things all at once. My hands clench him harder. Of their own accord, my muscles contract around him, as if they're determined to keep him inside me. My thoughts sizzle and evaporate like water on a frying pan, leaving only a darkness filled by the overwhelming sensation of his body moving in just the right way.

Short noises leave me, begging him, urging him to keep going.

His hand slips down between my body and the comforter, finding my ass and squeezing hard. A surge of pleasure goes through me, and in an instant, I'm over the edge. Fire rips through my veins, white-hot and leaving the world scoured clean in its wake. Every nerve I own sings. My muscles clench and ripple around him, and I cry out. I can't keep this bottled up. It's too amazing. I'm drowning in the feeling of him inside me.

His motions grow faster. He makes a wild sound, desperate and hungry, and his hands tighten on me for a few seconds before he slows again. I feel him twitching inside my body, a strange sensation that nevertheless makes me smile.

For a long moment, he lies on me. I can feel his heart pounding. His breaths come in short, ragged gasps. And then he pushes away to look down into my eyes.

"You're incredible," he whispers.

A blush tries to overwhelm the flush already heating my skin. That can't really be true. He *seems* like he means it, and the kindness of the words makes my heart flutter, but come on. I don't know anything.

I give an awkward shrug. "I'm just—"

His fingers brush my cheek, gently silencing my words. "Incredible." His fingertips move lower, tracing a line along my lips. Something almost pained drifts through his eyes. "*God*, so incredible."

He lies there for a moment, his gaze on my lips, and then he lets out a slow breath. Gently, he slips from inside me and then rolls away. He removes the condom, disposes of it somewhere on the far side of the bed, and then turns to the blanket folded down by our feet. Drawing it up, he spreads it over both of us, warming me against the air that has just started to turn cold on my sweat-coated skin. Lying back against the pillows, he slips his arm around my shoulders, pulling me close.

I snuggle up against him, my head on his chest and my naked body fitting so well to his side. Of its own accord, my leg wraps itself over his. It's instinctive, and for a moment, I worry he won't like it. But he just makes a contented noise and adjusts his arm to keep me there.

And it's surreal. Us. Together. All of it.

Surreal and wonderful.

My eyes drift shut, lulled by the sound of his heartbeat beneath me. I feel his hand find mine. Feel his thumb play along the side of my fingers. It's that same tender gesture —the one that always precedes him pulling away from me and shutting me out again.

I bite my lip, waiting.

Nothing happens. The motion continues on, running back and forth over my fingers, tracing gentle paths along the surface of my hands. His head turns a bit, and he kisses the top of my hair.

Tears sneak up on me out of nowhere, and it takes everything I have to hold them back. I don't know what I'm feeling. It's an ache, stabbing into my chest. It's a weight, crushing down on me. Because this moment is perfect. I want to wrap it up, protect it from the universe. From time. From life.

I never want it to end.

And I know it will. The whole world is waiting out there, full of terrible things that are trying to steal my best friend from me. We need to go back out to deal with them.

But in this one moment, in this one place, everything is so perfect.

I'm scared that too soon it'll shatter and all the tiny, precious pieces will fall.

2 3

WE LIE IN BED FOR ANOTHER FEW MINUTES BEFORE I FEEL Amar move beside me. "Hey," he says quietly.

I look up toward him.

"You never had anything to eat today, did you?"

My brow furrows. I suppose I haven't. It's been madness since last night, though. My appetite has totally checked out.

He shifts around as if to rise. I push away to give him room.

"Come on." He nods toward the door and then stops. "Unless you want a shower first?"

I start to shrug, but then his brow twitches up. I pause. Oh. A shower. Like…

In tingles and throbs, my body begins waking up all over again. My imagination runs ahead of me, nodding a frantic yes while pelting my brain with visions of what showering with this man would be like.

My stomach chooses that moment to growl.

We both freeze. Mortification shoots through me, but Amar only laughs. "I guess that decides it."

He rolls over while I curse my stomach for its treachery. My God, it couldn't have held out a *little* while longer?

Amar pushes the blanket back, climbing from the bed, and my annoyance drains fast. Naked, he walks to his closet to retrieve some clothes from inside. I don't move, letting my eyes roam over the muscular lines of his back, his legs, his ass. Amazement bubbles up in me all over again for what's happened between us.

He turns and catches sight of me watching him. A blush burns its way up my face. He grins.

I drop my gaze away, my heart doing a weird flutter thing that makes it hard to breathe. God, I love his smile.

Amar pulls on a pair of drawstring pants. Taking a shirt from the closet, he comes back toward the bed and extends it to me. I take it from him with a murmur of thanks.

I tug the shirt over my head. It's soft, well-worn cotton with our university logo on the front, and when I rise from the bed, it hangs down by my thighs. I retrieve my panties from the floor, pull them on as well, and then pad along the dark carpet after him in my bare feet.

In the kitchen, he flips on a light and then gestures to the breakfast bar and the tall stools arranged in front of it. "Have a seat," he offers.

Wait, he's going to cook? For me?

Amar gives me an insistent look. "Please?"

Cold wood chills my bare legs when I sink onto the stool. I watch while he heads for the fridge and takes a carton of eggs from inside. He really doesn't have to do this. I've been cooking for myself for years.

It's sort of strange to have someone do that for me now.

"Omelet okay?" he asks.

"I can help."

He pauses in this odd way that instantly makes me regret the words.

"Yeah," I amend quickly. "Thank you."

He nods and turns back to the counter. I study him while he sets to cracking the eggs into a metal bowl. He's enjoying himself, I realize. Like, in a way I've never seen from him.

Bracing my elbow on the black marble breakfast bar, I rest my chin in my hand. I wonder if he's ever done this before. Cooked for somebody.

Something inside me suspects maybe not.

The corner of my mouth rises in a smile.

"So do you like—what?" Amar turns back and spots my expression.

"Nothing." I shake my head, wiping the smile from my face. "What's the question?"

"Are cheese and pepper okay?"

I nod. He echoes the motion and then goes to the cabinet, taking a pepper shaker from inside. My smile creeps back. I bury it fast, looking away.

My gaze finds the windows on the far side of the room. The sunlight streaming through them is slightly dimmed by the reflective coating on the glass, but I can still see the blue sky dotted by white puffs of clouds.

I wonder what time it is.

The thought brings back worry like a rising flood. I glance around, searching for a clock. Above the stove, I spot one, and my stomach flip-flops. It's later than I thought.

No one has called yet.

Guilt like acid begins to chew a path through every good thing that's just happened. I shouldn't have stopped, not even for a second. I know I'm trying to trust Amar, but I shouldn't have—

"Hey," he says gently.

I blink and glance back at him. He's watching me, concern in his eyes like he knows what's running through my head.

"Someone will call," he promises. "We'll find her."

It's difficult to believe the words, no matter how much I want to. Swallowing hard, I make myself nod and push away the worry as best I can. I'm not going to ruin this.

"Thank you," I manage. "For, you know, hiring…"

I don't know how to finish the sentence. God knows who—or what—he hired.

Amar nods. "Of course."

He returns the remaining eggs to the fridge. Silence stretches, more uncomfortable than before.

"So your, um, your apartment's nice," I try desperately.

Amar hesitates, that weird, closed-off look coming back to his expression.

My heart sinks. Dammit, no. What'd I do?

"It's all right," he allows.

I don't know what to say.

The stone-like cast to his face cracks. "It works for what I need. It all comes from my father's money, though. I inherited what he had when he died."

My stomach churns, the reason behind his reaction suddenly clicking. His father, the guy who ripped him away from his home and put him through who knew what. And I just inadvertently brought the bastard up. "I'm sorry, I didn't mean—"

"I know." His tone is softer than before. He sighs. "It's fine. Just take care of yourself, okay? Eat. Keep your energy up."

I nod. I know he's right. I'm no good to anyone if I'm falling over from hunger.

Speaking of hunger, though…

"What is it?" he asks.

"Mist. I don't remember any when we, you know…" I twitch my head toward the bedroom.

He suddenly seems uncomfortable.

"What?" I ask.

"You were, but I didn't take it in."

I stare at him, baffled. "But—" I don't know where to begin. "You weren't, though? And you didn't—"

"We can't."

My confusion gets stronger. "Can't?"

"We can't feed from each other. Ever."

I feel a shiver building up inside me. "The club, though. Last night, when you—"

"That was different." He looks like the words are being pulled from him. "I was careful—*very*—and I only gave you a little bit. Just enough to snap you out of it."

I fight to keep my expression from becoming incredulous. That was a *bit*? "And if you'd given me more?"

"It could have been bad."

I'm flabbergasted. "What does that mean?"

Exhaling, Amar sets down the metal bowl in his hand. "It means it's dangerous. For full-bloods, taking in the mist of another incubus or succubus like that is nauseating, like food poisoning. But for Legacies, to let our human sides out, to let one of our own feed us their magic… it can change things inside us. Damage us." He hesitates, something almost like an apology flickering over his face. "It could turn us, Cait. Make us into Touched too."

A breath rushes from my chest. I feel like I've been

punched in the gut. But... of course it would. We're half-human, and to be fed mist from a demon...

Appearing discomfited, Amar returns to the stove and continues working on the omelets.

I look away, the implications ricocheting through me. We need energy—sexual energy—to survive, and getting it from each other... we can't. Because it'll turn us into *that*, we can't.

Ever.

I swallow hard. So that means other people. Both of us, other people, no matter what there is between Amar and me. And that won't ever change.

The good just keeps slipping away, no matter how I try to hold onto it.

I draw in a lungful of air, struggling to fight back the ache in my chest. I'm being ridiculous. I should have expected this. I mean, sure, I want there to be more between us. I would *love* there to be more between us. But it's not like Amar ever promised anything. Some committed relationship or whatever. For that matter, Bianca acted like it was a foregone conclusion, the fact that I'd end up sleeping with as many people as I could get my hands on. And sure, I'd chalked some—*most*—of that up to her demonic hatred of anything romantic, but still.

I should have seen this coming. Something like this, anyway.

A plate appears in front of me. I blink, tugging my gaze from the window. I don't know how long I've been sitting here, staring out at the city and the sky without seeing a bit of it. I force a smile onto my face. "Thanks."

Amar nods. I attempt to ignore the way his eyes linger on me, like he's trying to figure out what I thought about what he said. Picking up the fork he set next to the food, I begin cutting into the omelet.

A moment passes before he joins me, taking the seat beside me with a plate of his own.

I lock my gaze on the countertop, doing everything I can to ignore the tension between us. I don't know how to fix this. What to say.

I wish I'd never asked about the damn mist.

Fighting to bury how this hurts—from myself as much as him—I take a bite of the food. Flavors of spices, cheese, and egg melt in my mouth. I blink.

"Oh wow," I mumble and then swallow. "This is incredible."

He shrugs.

"No, seriously."

A smile twitches his lip. "I'm glad you like it."

I nod, and then an idea occurs to me, shining and desperate and hopeful like it's delivered from above. I know it doesn't *fix* anything—not the mist or what we are, anyway—but maybe, just maybe, it can still save this moment. Still give us a shot at something resembling normalcy.

"I do," I assure him. "But, um, what would you think about us maybe cooking together sometime too? Like, dinner?"

I don't even breathe, waiting for his response.

His expression turns softer. His smile grows. "I'd like that."

A grin bubbles up in me, brought about by that incredible smile.

In the bedroom, his cell phone rings.

For a moment, neither of us moves, and then he pushes

away from the stool and strides back down the hall. I stay on the chair, paralyzed.

I hear his voice, low and muffled, and then silence.

Amar walks back out to the living room. "That was Brett."

His face is somber. I make myself keep breathing.

"He thinks they've found something."

I barely remember rushing to leave Amar's apartment or yanking on my borrowed clothes and strappy sandals. I barely even remember shadow-crossing.

We appear in an alley near Temptation, and immediately, I'm moving, jogging from the narrow passage and on toward the front entrance to the nightclub. The sidewalk is practically empty compared to the bustle I saw when Temptation is open. A few cars drive down the street on their way someplace else, and the only businesses in the area are the type that open by appointment only.

"Cait," Amar calls from behind me.

I look over my shoulder.

He's stopped several yards back, by the alley leading to the rear entrance. "This way."

Reversing my path, I rush past him toward the rear of the club. Now that I have a destination, a target, I hate every second that's stretching between me and the moment when we've finally rescued Ruby. Amar strides after me, his long legs chewing up the distance between us and bringing him back to my side.

Beyond the weathered posters for local bands covering the bricks, a symbol glows on the wall. Foggy memory comes back to me, and in spite of myself, I circle wide. I saw that thing the night this all started, burning on the wall with no source to give it light.

"It's nothing," Amar says, seeing my trepidation. "Demon marking. Tells our kind this is a safe place to feed. Humans just see graffiti."

I balk at the words. Lovely.

Blinking fast, I keep going. There's a plain steel door against the wall opposite from the symbol, its surface dented like someone tried to bash it in. I don't remember the damage from the other night when I raced by it on my way out of the club, but then, some parts of that night are still a blur.

Amar pauses short of the step leading to the entrance. He knocks twice and waits. I can't stop fidgeting. My eyes dart up and down the alley. The seconds keep bleeding away.

The latch clicks, and then the door swings toward us. "Well, you made good time," comments the guy standing beyond the opening.

Amar doesn't respond, and the guy grins. He steps aside to let us both enter, and I eye him askance while we walk into the club. This has to be Bianca's brother, Brett. He looks several years older than her, but he's got the same shade of blond hair and blue eyes. Something about the way he speaks reminds me of her too: like nothing quite matters, so why should he care? He's tall, almost Amar's height, with a bearing that makes it nearly impossible to imagine he's not solid muscle. Unlike his sister, though, his clothes don't radiate money. In jeans and a flannel shirt with the sleeves rolled up, he seems more like a cleaned-up construction worker than the owner of one of the most popular nightclubs in town.

"Are you Cait?" he asks.

I nod, wondering if his sister said anything about me.

And how bad what she said might've been.

"Uh, yeah. You're Brett?"

"Yep. Nice to meet you." He glances back toward the club. Most of the lights are dimmed or turned off entirely, leaving the dance floor a black pit and making the level around us feel like an empty theater stage. Through the hall leading to the bar and the front door, I can see the glow of brighter lights, though not much of the illumination reaches this far. "So, listen," he continues to Amar. "I had one of the packs head to your place to keep an eye out, just in case Volgert gets twitchy and thinks you're bringing the girl there. But the others'll be here soon, so if you want to find you and Cait a place up in the office, Rafael can get you both whatever you need till we bring the girl—"

"Wait, what?" I cut in. "I'm going with you."

Brett's brow climbs.

"You can't," Amar says.

I stare at him. I have no idea what they're talking about —packs and taking Ruby to Amar's place—but I can read this part on his face. He planned this. He had no intention of bringing me beyond this point.

"This is the safest place for us right now," Amar continues. "Rafael will—"

"No," I protest, "I need to—"

"You *need* to take care of yourself. These people are incredibly dangerous—"

"I don't care!"

Amar's jaw tightens.

"Dude," Brett comments. "What's gotten into you? It's her friend; it's her call. It's not like she's in the same situation as you."

I look between them in confusion. What situation?

Amar glances at Brett. Everything seems to die in his expression. "Then I'm coming too."

Brett scoffs incredulously. "*What?* Man, Bianca said you were being reckless, but you can't seriously—"

"Cait can't defend herself."

"So? How's that *your* problem? Besides, I heard she blew up some stuff at Bianca's place just fine the other day."

"By accident."

I try not to appear uncomfortable, but they're talking about me like I'm not even here.

And about how I'm incompetent, no less.

"You want to be the only one who can fight if this gets ugly?" Amar continues.

Brett hesitates, his eyes flicking over Amar, and for only a heartbeat, his face goes inscrutable. But then he simply shrugs. "Fine. Whatever. Your funeral."

I look at Amar, but he doesn't react to the turn of phrase. Without another word, he strides toward the lighted hall on the other side of the gallery.

"So you charged up enough for the rest of it?"

I blink and pull my attention to Brett. "What?"

"You *are* still going to be the one who tries to bring her back from this, right? Assuming it's possible, anyway. I mean, she's your friend, so you'll probably have the best shot, but odds like that..." He shrugs his brow illustratively.

"What odds?"

Confusion crosses his face. "Amar didn't—" Brett regroups. "Never mind. It's cool. You saved that girl at the hospital, so you'll probably get lucky this time too."

"Wait, *what*?"

His phone buzzes, saving him from answering me. Drawing it out quickly, he glances down. "The others are here."

He starts for the door. I grab his arm, stopping him. "What do you mean?"

Reluctance on his face, Brett extracts his arm from my grasp. "Only about five percent of the Touched are ever brought back from it. The rest never recover. Their minds are too far gone."

I stare after him, speechless, while he walks out of the room.

∞

THE "OTHERS" CONSIST OF FOUR MEN AND TWO WOMEN WHO all look like bikers—leather vests, tattoos, and all.

Plus, the motorcycles help.

Amar doesn't look at me while we walk from the alleyway entrance to meet them. He seems to have shut himself off from the world completely. It's like I don't even exist anymore.

I want to scream at him. For that, for his silence. For *all* of his goddamn silences, and how he hid this latest piece of utter nightmare news. Five percent. *Five* percent. That's... that's almost *nothing*. That's practically no chance at—

I close my eyes briefly and keep walking toward the road, but it's a struggle to make myself concentrate. It's like the number is emblazoned in my mind. I'd figured saving Ruby from being Touched was a given—I saved that girl in the hospital, after all. I didn't think it was *that* incredible.

No wonder I'd drawn so much attention.

I fight that thought off too. Amar hadn't told me. He hadn't and he should have.

But would I have wanted to know?

I exhale sharply. I can't answer that. But it doesn't matter. Even if I don't know what I did at the hospital before, even if the odds are small, I'll save Ruby. *We'll* save her.

There's no way Ruby is too far gone.

The bikers give us a cursory glance while we come closer. Between the four guys, their skin ranges from pale to dark while their builds are muscular to the point they're unnerving. Somehow, I get the impression the guy closest to us is in charge. I'm not sure why. Maybe it's just the fact his bike has stopped slightly ahead of the others.

The women aren't much different. One of them has amber-toned skin while the other is white, but otherwise, they're the same. Cold faces, dark hair. They look like they eat concrete for breakfast. Women and men alike, the group spares me a perfunctory glance, and then they're focused on Brett with this strange, laser-like intensity.

"Forest Service storage facility west of Glacy Park," Brett tells them. "Unit A-Six."

The group is silent, and Brett doesn't seem to expect a response. He simply glances at Amar, who twitches his head toward a gunmetal-colored sports car parked several yards away.

"I'll drive," Amar offers flatly.

Brett shrugs and then digs some keys from his pocket.

He tosses them to Amar, who catches them effortlessly before walking toward the car.

We follow him. The bikers' eyes stay on us while Amar starts the engine, and only when he pulls away from the curb does the guy up front motion to the others. The roar of the motorcycles rings from the walls of the businesses around us.

I struggle not to fidget in the narrow back seat, watching the biker group lead the way down the road. "What are they?" I ask. I know they're not human. It wouldn't have occurred to me a week or so ago—hell, it might not have occurred to me a *day* ago—but now... oh yeah. Something about them just screams it.

Brett looks back to me when Amar doesn't say anything. Demon or not, he's more personable than his sister, I realize, by about a hundredfold. Instead of the derisive look Bianca would undoubtedly have given me, he seems like he thinks the question is a nice diversion from the boring drive.

"Werewolves."

I blink. Out of nowhere, I'm hit with the overwhelming urge to laugh.

Oh. Of course they are.

I fight back any trace of expression. "Werewolves?" I hear myself repeat.

Amusement crosses Brett's face like he saw my surprise anyway. "Yeah. Their kind keep to themselves mostly, but if you pay them enough..." He shrugs, and then his face turns wry. "They're berserkers in a fight, though. Be sure you stay out of their way."

I shiver. My gaze twitches to Amar. "So they're some of the, um, people you hired?"

I struggle with the word despite knowing it's the only

one to use. If I'm a succubus and a person, werewolves have to be people as well.

Brett looks puzzled when Amar doesn't respond. "Nah, Bianca hired these. She got three different packs last night to work on finding your friend."

His cell buzzes, and he turns back to take the call. I don't move, still processing his words. I've been fairly certain that girl might hate me, or at least that she's only done the bare minimum so far, and only because Amar asked her to. And maybe that's the case. Maybe three packs of mercenary werewolves are nothing in her world.

Maybe…

We continue through town and out past the city limits. The car winds through the hills, and no matter how much I might like to pretend otherwise, I know the flip-flopping of my stomach has nothing to do with the twisting terrain.

But then, it's going to be okay. Ruby will be there. I know it. And we'll save her.

The sports car slows, and I look up. Ahead of us, the bikers have come to a stop at a turn for a side road. A chain strung between two cement posts blocks the path, and a metal sign hangs from it, warning everyone that this is a road for service vehicles only. The lead biker jerks his head at one of the others, who gets off his motorcycle. He draws something from the bag on the side of his bike and then approaches the chain. Swiftly, he cuts through the metal.

We follow the six of them past the cement posts. The fallen sign clunks beneath the car when we drive over it.

I shift position uncomfortably on the back seat. I can feel my skin tingling, like whatever the hell it is I have inside me is a heartbeat from blowing something up.

Seconds crawl past. Gravel rumbles under the tires in a monotonous drone.

The others pull over. Amar does the same. The bikers wait till we leave the car to get off their motorcycles.

I can't tell what's going on. Brett simply nods at them, and then they turn, the six of them slipping into the woods.

My eyes dart between them, Brett, and Amar. "What —" I start to whisper.

I cut off at Amar's sharp glance.

"Checking the area," Brett whispers, his voice so low I can barely make out the words. He puts a finger to his lips, motioning for my silence.

I look back to the forest, feeling like an idiot. Reconnaissance. Right.

Minutes tick past. I'm crawling out of my skin. Surely, we should have heard something by now. Moved on by now.

Leaves rustle. My attention snaps to the left, and I spot one of the women stepping from the bushes, her hand on a branch to push it aside.

She let it make noise intentionally. She must have. I didn't hear a thing till she was right on top of us.

The shivers inside my skin grow stronger.

Her dark eyes flick to me and then back to Brett, her expression somber.

My heart climbs my throat. I clench my arms to me tighter, fighting the urge to demand to know what the hell they've found. The woman twitches her head back the way she's come and then disappears into the bushes again, not making a sound.

Brett and Amar are already striding toward the car. I look from them to the space where the woman had been and then hurry toward the vehicle and scramble into the back seat. Amar puts the car into gear. Neither of them say a word.

The ride is short. The car pulls around a turn after only two minutes, and a clearing opens up ahead of us. A rusted warehouse occupies most of the space, and flaking red paint on the green siding identifies the building as A-Six. When we come to a stop, I spot three of the bikers leaving the building through a metal door while several of the rest are simply waiting in the gravel parking lot.

But I don't see Ruby. I don't see anyone else.

I climb from the car, my body shaking.

The lead biker walks toward us, and I struggle not to take a step back. He's even larger up close. "They're gone," he says. "Hour ago or more from the smell of it."

Brett mutters a curse.

I stare at them all. "So… now what?"

The words are desperate. Breathy. I sound like a kid, and I hate it, but that's not the most important thing right now. Ruby should have been here. *Was* here.

If we'd only been a little faster…

Brett looks at Amar. "I'll make some calls."

I choke on a shriek. Calls. Goddamn, *fucking* phone calls. If I hadn't stopped looking, if we'd just been a *little* faster—

My feet are moving before I register the impulse. I race toward the building.

"Cait!" Amar protests.

I don't look back. The werewolves melt from my path. The doorway falls behind me, and an acrid stench hits my nose, making my eyes water. Shadows engulf the place. Only a narrow window at the peak of the wall behind me saves the room from being pitch black.

Bulky shapes line the floor. Square shapes, maybe six

feet long, but nowhere near that high. I can't make out what they are.

"Dammit," Amar snaps, coming up behind me. "They could have traps in here."

I hesitate on the verge of stepping farther into the room. "What is this?" I ask, not taking my eyes from the strange objects.

Silence follows. Anger surges up in me. He can't keep things from me again. Not here. Not now.

"Cages," comes a gravelly voice at my back.

I turn. The lead biker stands at the entrance, silhouetted by the light from outside.

"W-what?" I stammer.

The man pauses. "Cages for the Touched."

I feel sick.

"No women were in this place," the guy continues. "Three men—two dead, one gone. But no women. She wasn't being kept here."

My gorge rises fast, the reason for the stench suddenly hitting me. I retreat from the room quickly, choking down the nausea clawing up my throat.

Amar follows me.

I don't look back at him. The forest air clears my head, but it does nothing for how I can't seem to stop shaking. I don't know what's worse: the fact we might've missed her, or the fact she'd never been here at all.

Tears burn in my eyes.

"We'll find her," Amar promises quietly.

I shake my head. I don't want to hear the rest. I *know* the rest; he's been saying it since last night. My gaze skips across the clearing, trying to find hope amid the utter pointlessness of this entire trip.

There's nothing. By the car, Brett is on his phone. The

other bikers are standing around the clearing, watching the forest and us alike.

My eyes lift to the sky. The sun is still high above the treetops, but it's already creeping toward afternoon. A few more hours, and it'll be sundown.

"Oh my God, Ruby," I whisper. "Where are you?"

2 5

RUBY

IT'S DIFFICULT TO SEE ANYMORE, DIFFICULT TO FEEL ANYTHING but the cold. The world is a blur of light and shadow, concrete and steel, all of it frigid and aching and filled with a hunger she can't shake. She doesn't know how long she's been here. Hours? Years? Time has no meaning. It's hard to even care. They moved her a few times, she knows, shifting her out of this box, putting her in others, and for a while, there'd been another girl. Some other girl they'd brought into the cell, dumping her onto the floor like a bag of garbage, leaving her when they closed the door.

She doesn't know what happened to that girl.

But the big guy hasn't been back in a while, and it hurts. She hurts. He reappeared briefly sometime after they brought the girl, delivering a burst of hot, world-erasing ecstasy that ended entirely too soon. And now her whole body aches, desperate for the moment he comes back again.

Her fingers paw absently at the rough floor. Red-brown flakes encrust her hands. Her arms. Her shirt. She can't remember why.

She wonders where the other girl went.

Footsteps thud on the floor. Her head snaps up, her gaze pinning itself on the door at the sound.

He's here again.

She's across the cell in a heartbeat, her face pressed to the opening. Her hands stretch past the bars, clawing at him, craving his touch.

But it doesn't come. Standing too far from her, he watches while she moans and begs without words for him to come closer.

And he smiles.

"You have to earn it now, little one," he chides her. "And you will. Soon."

TIME WAS INVENTED BY A DEVIL OR AN ANGEL, AND I CAN'T figure out which. I'm desperate for the hours to slow down. To understand and be merciful, giving us space to find her.

And I'm begging them to stop torturing me and just race ahead till sunset so we can leave for the wharf. At least that's one place I know Ruby will be.

Except that's where she might die.

Pressing my hand to my face, I continue pacing the end of Brett's office. It's a long room with wood-paneled walls on three sides and mirrored windows on the other, the latter of which overlook the dance floor. The room itself doesn't appear much like a nightclub owner's office. Like Brett, it seems as if it'd be more at home on a construction site. It's invisible when the club is open—lost in the shadows above the lasers and lights—but now it's a bright spot on the black wall and makes me feel like we're in a fishbowl.

One whose only other feature is an endlessly ticking clock.

For the thousandth time, I force my attention away while I pass the clock. It sends nausea into my throat every time I see it. I can't stare at it anymore.

My fingers clench around my cell. I've been carrying it all afternoon, flinching whenever I think it buzzes—though I've been wrong each time. I've even made a few calls of my own, trying to reach Kyle, trying to do anything. But it's useless. Kyle hasn't answered. I can practically hear the bastard laughing at me.

And House Volgert is probably laughing as well. In the past several hours, Amar and Bianca's people have come across five more places where Touched were kept. Five more dank little holes with cages and cold cement. The bikers hadn't even bothered calling till after they investigated, though. Even from a distance, they were able to tell the places had been abandoned.

I circle an island of file boxes and start my circuit again.

"Cait."

I look at Amar, alarm freezing me. "What?"

"You should head back to Bianca's."

"Huh? Why?"

He hesitates. "It's almost sunset."

My eyes flash to the clock. Holy shit.

I'm fairly certain the devils and angels are laughing at me too.

"No." I shake my head. "I'm going with you."

Amar grimaces. "Cait." His voice is stressed. "Please."

"It's not smart," Brett adds. "They know you want your friend back. If you show up there—"

"They'll be watching me. I know."

Brett gives me a skeptical look. "Well, then—"

"Can that *help*?" I press. "If I… I mean, if I *distract* them, maybe you could—"

"No." Amar appears deadly.

"But if you had the werewolves—"

Brett makes a rude sound. "They're mercenaries. They're good for grunt work, but they don't give a crap about anyone's *safety*. You're better off heading back—"

"Dammit, I'm not going to just—"

"Cait," Amar starts.

"I'm not having this argument again!"

They both pause at my shout. Amar seems cold and furious, while Brett's eyebrow just twitches up.

"I can be a distraction," I continue, forcing my voice to be calmer. "Amar can too. The people who have Ruby are just as likely to be on guard when they see him as when they see me."

Brett's mouth tightens like he's already had that thought. His eyes skirt toward Amar as if he wants to insist he stay behind as well.

I take a breath at the sight. "Besides," I continue, "you need someone who knows what she looks like. We're the only two who can do that—and I can do it better than him."

My head twitches to Amar, but I don't look his way. My gaze is fixed on Brett. He's easier to focus on.

And I can imagine what I'll see on Amar's face.

Brett shakes his head. "Fine," he scoffs, and for a moment, he could be Bianca's twin. "I'll call the mercenaries. Let them know that, apparently, you're going kamikaze mode."

Rolling his eyes, he walks away. His expression makes

my blood boil. I know this is dangerous, but I also know I'm right. I can identify Ruby—no matter *what*, I can.

I'm not bailing on her now.

Amar doesn't say a word. He almost doesn't need to. I can feel his anger at my plan rolling off him in waves.

But I don't care. I *can't* care.

Avoiding his gaze, I escape toward the door.

❦

TERCHETT WHARF SHOULD HAVE BEEN TORN DOWN YEARS ago. A hulking complex of warehouses that primarily seems comprised of rust, faded paint, and less-faded graffiti, the structures back up on an inlet of the Puloxi River. Most of the city locals wonder at the fact it still stands.

Now I wonder if the Houses were behind that.

We step from a shadow and appear at the exit of a viaduct several hundred yards from the wharf. We left the car back at Temptation, under the assumption we'd probably need to leave this place faster than the vehicle would allow.

The reality of that does nothing for the butterflies in my stomach.

I hold myself as calmly and determinedly as I can manage, even though my back muscles are cramping with nervousness and my heart seems hell-bent on pounding itself out of my chest. Beside me, Amar looks like he does this all the time, like he's gone utterly calm in the time it took us to travel from Brett's place.

It's weird.

Motorcycles growl in the twilight, and a moment later, the bikers arrive, pulling to a stop on the stretch of broken concrete that fronts the main building. It's only one pack, though. Others hired by Bianca and Amar alike have circled somewhere behind the building, searching for Ruby and an alternate way inside, while still more are surrounding the wharf in case they need to cover our retreat. The werewolves don't spare us a glance while they swing off their bikes and head for the door, but something inside me can't quite be convinced they don't know we're here.

I shiver in the cool evening air. I want to run for the door right now, though I know we're supposed to give them a few moments. Brett stayed behind specifically to keep Volgert from becoming suspicious that Amar and I had anyone helping us tonight. It's no good screwing that up now.

The waiting is killing me.

I straighten my shoulders, struggling to will my shivering to subside. It'll be fine. *She'll* be fine. Soon this'll be just a bad memory.

"Cait."

I tense at the sound of Amar's voice. He hasn't tried to argue me out of this since my outburst at Temptation. I hope he doesn't start now.

"What?" I reply, not looking at him.

"You can't show any reaction in there. Nothing. No matter what you see. No matter what anyone says. This isn't like the vampires. You won't survive it here."

That pulls my eyes toward him. That and his tone, almost like—if he were anyone else—he'd be begging.

His expression gives no sign of it, though. Chills run through me at the utterly solemn look in his eyes.

"You have to be cold, Cait," he continues quietly. "Cold

as you've ever been in your life. If they think you're like a human, they'll eat you alive."

I manage a nod.

Amar echoes the motion and then starts toward the building. My heart tries to follow by way of my throat.

Swallowing hard, I trail him toward the massive doors at the side of the warehouse. The things look medieval. They're made of metal, easily twice as tall as Amar, and arched like a pair of castle gates. I can't imagine what purpose they must have served when this place was just a warehouse, though maybe the Houses put them in after the fact. They're rusted and plastered with signs warning that trespassing is forbidden, but glowing glyphs dot the space between the signs, a tangle of multicolored symbols I can't hope to decipher. Metal bars cross the gates, reinforcing the medieval image, though disturbingly, I realize they're on the wrong side of the door. The bars would trap people *in* the building, not keep them out.

The butterflies in my stomach turn to bees, ricocheting from my insides and making me want to throw up.

Two men step from the shadows on either side of the enormous door. They're huge and look like they probably dreamed of joining professional wrestling as children. With their arms crossed over their leather jackets, they eye us as if they're accustomed to causing pain and prepared to do it again.

"Let us in," Amar says calmly.

The guy on the left smirks. His gaze runs over Amar like he sees something that amuses him. After a moment's consideration, though, he gestures to a smaller door behind them, its square shape nearly lost on the dark surface of the larger gate.

Amar starts forward only to stop when neither man

moves from his path. The left guy's smirk grows, and another moment passes before he and his buddy finally step back, barely giving us enough room to walk through.

I stick close behind Amar, skirting between the two bouncers and doing everything I can to keep from brushing them accidentally. The air feels charged, like if I touch them, it'll explode.

Amar doesn't spare them a backward glance. Tugging open the door, he holds it for me to pass him and then drops it closed behind us, sealing us in darkness.

But it's not empty. Strange sounds fill the black. Howls, wails, and shouts coming from a distance I can't see.

It sounds like hell. My heart is pounding so hard, I think it's going to batter its way out of my chest. I choke down a gulp of the clammy air, fighting to keep from panicking.

"Cait."

My breath catches at Amar's whisper, barely audible over the far-off noise. His hand finds mine. The simple contact is reassuring. My racing heart starts to slow.

I feel his warmth when he comes closer, and his breath brushes my ear when he speaks. "You can still leave."

My head shakes. "No."

For a moment, his hand stays in mine. Air escapes him, however. In the sound, I can hear the frustration that must be reflected on his face.

"Okay," he surrenders. His hand slips away. "Just... don't forget what I said outside. Please."

I nod, though I'm aware he can't see me. I wish he'd take my hand again, even if I know he can't. It's stupid. I'm not a child. I can handle this.

A howl carries down the hall, followed by cheers, and

nausea scrambles up my throat. Amar's footsteps start away. I hurry after him.

The noise grows louder. The darkness begins to fade, turning to a creepy twilight of rotting wooden floors and rough walls dripping with condensation. We round a corner, and a room opens up ahead of us, filled with people standing below bare light bulbs strung on industrial-looking cords. The crowd has their backs to us. They're looking at something farther on.

That changes when Amar reaches the entrance. People glance over and then step aside. I see eyes trailing us while we walk forward, the crowd's attention refocusing on us both.

But mostly on him, not me.

My attention darts around. I'm scarcely drawing notice, really. One or two people stare at me, their eyes tracking me with unnerving intensity, but the rest watch Amar. They're gaping like they recognize him, like they can't believe he's here. Gazes of every color from ordinary brown and blue to silver or red lock on him, alarm reflected in every one. But only a few of their owners look human. I see fangs, pointed ears, and a man with what I'd swear are knife slices filled by *metal* on his face. And everyone is too close. Anybody could just reach out and—

The mass of people opens up ahead of us, and my thoughts stutter to a stop. Several steps ahead, the floor drops away to a pit at least a dozen feet deep and a good thirty feet wide. The sides are paneled with splintered wood and topped by enough barbed wire to stop a charging bull. A rope ladder hangs from the far side, giving the people above access to the pit below. Dirt covers the floor, and when we draw closer, I can see that's not all.

A man lies on the right side of the pit, a dark red trail

across the dirt behind him like he's been dragged there. He's covered in blood, from his torn button-down shirt to his stained khaki pants, and his face is a mess of deep gouges and scrapes. He's sprawled out, his chest heaving for air and his midsection spasming like his tattered shirt is the only thing holding him together.

He's not alone. I recognize the brown ponytail of the guy crouched with his back to us. The wounded man's upper body rests on the lap of the girl we met earlier today.

Leaf doesn't turn around, but Blue looks up like she can feel my attention. Her skin is paler than it was this morning, almost like it's turned to snow, and her eyes glint like brilliant blue topazes. In glossy waves, her brown hair reflects the glow from the utility lights overhead while her black clothes just seem to absorb it completely. Her lips are parted. Fangs glint between them.

The man starts to wail. His hands claw at the dirt, and his body jerks like it's tearing itself apart from the inside.

Blue's focus returns to him immediately. I see her mouth move when she says something to him, her expression becoming kind. She strokes his face as if he's a sick child, and then she bends over him while Leaf does the same.

I tear my gaze away. I can't watch this. Oh my God, they're—

My eyes land on the other side of the pit. A man is there, clutching the barbed wire and hanging from it, ignoring the way it has cut into his hands. Below him, a ring of muscled guys are watching with cattle prods in their meaty fists. Something in their stances makes me think they're meant to keep him under control. The guy doesn't pay them any attention, though. He's just dangling like a monkey from the barbed wire, his face upturned, his mouth gasping, utter ecstasy painted across his blood-splattered face. But above him, another man is crouched at the edge of the pit.

Mist is pouring from his palm and down over the first guy's face.

Like he's feeding it to him.

I choke, and it takes everything I have to keep my feet rooted to the ground. I want to run. I want to shout for Ruby. But that's not the plan. I have to stick to the plan.

Shaking, I tug my attention from him too, forcing it to the area beyond the crowd on the other side of the pit. The bikers will be in here, somewhere. By the massive gate I can see on the opposite end of the room, maybe. After all, their job is to scope out the entrance to the place where Volgert is keeping the Touched, while the rest of the mercenaries find a way in from the outside. And then they'll buzz Amar's cell. Tell us to come meet them once the guards around the Touched are neutralized.

Any minute now…

Adrenaline pounds through my veins while I scan the enormous room. This place must have been a warehouse floor at some point, though who knows why there's a humongous pit in the middle. Work of the Houses, again, maybe—though really, it's not important.

Seriously, *any* minute would be good…

People are still staring. Several of them have started circling either side of the pit, heading toward us with looks on their faces like they're going to haul us out of here in pieces. But that's okay. Our job is to make them think we're the only ones here for Ruby. To make them focus on us so they won't notice anything else.

No one told me it was going to work *this* well.

"Amar…" I murmur.

"Remember what I told you," he replies, his voice completely calm. He doesn't take his eyes from the people coming toward us.

I tremble, but I still draw myself up straight, fighting to fasten the coldest and most uncaring expression on my face that I can.

It doesn't come easily. Those guys are gigantic. One of them is grinning. His teeth look like they're made of steel.

I drag my attention away from his mouth only to freeze at the sight of his face. I recognize him. He was the guy by the river. The one watching us after we met with Blue and Leaf.

Metal-teeth sees me staring at him. His grin widens. His bald head nods like he can just picture ripping me apart, and then he turns his eyes toward the far side of the room. My heart racing, I follow his gaze, but there's nothing. The crowd, eyeing us warily. The gate, still sealed and impenetrable. Does this guy know the werewolves are back there, trying to find a way in? Why is he—

The gate explodes.

Amar grabs me, moving faster than I can even understand, and next thing I know, I'm on my knees. He's over me. Covering me. I hear screams. People crying out in fear and pain, but I can't see anything. Nothing more than legs and rotting wood, anyway—all of it fogged by the dust now filling the air.

Just as quickly as he pushed me to the ground, Amar hauls me back upright, saving us both from getting trampled by the horde now fleeing toward the exit. But he doesn't head the same way, and he doesn't move for the gate either. Instead, he grips my arm hard and takes off through the crowd. People bump me, elbow me, blur in front of me: an endless mob rushing for an escape. I catch a glimpse of metal bars protruding from the destroyed wood-slat walls—bars that had been part of the gate only a few moments ago.

And some of them are wet. Bloody and dripping, like they hit people on their ballistic path across the room.

I want to throw up.

Howling rises above the shouting, and I look back.

A gap opens in the crowd. A wolf is at the heart of it, and the thing is massive. Its muzzle is stained red, and its eyes glow amber like a fire is trapped inside. Behind it, the space where the gate had been is nothing but rubble and boards caved in from the ceiling above. I can't see any way past them.

The wolf snarls and then leaps away. I hear more screaming.

Amar stops. We've reached a wall. There's a door, small and dark amid the rough wood paneling. He grabs the knob, twists it sharply, and a surge of weirdly cold static stings my arm where his hand holds me.

Something shatters inside the wood, and cracks run through the surface while, above the knob, the lock falls to pieces. The door opens. Amar yanks me through the gap, and I catch sight of the crumpled brass knob before he slams the door behind us.

Darkness engulfs us again. The air stinks of rotting wood, musty sweat, and who knows what else.

Amar's grip shifts. His other hand takes my shoulder, like he's turned to stand in front of me. "Are you all right?" he demands.

"Yeah." My voice is choked. I swallow hard, attempting to sound more confident. "Yeah, you?"

"Fine." His grip on my shoulder vanishes, but his hand

on my other arm doesn't leave. Pulling me with him, he starts into the darkness.

I draw a ragged breath and follow, hoping he knows where he's going. Hoping maybe one of his apparent superpowers is seeing in the dark.

Shivers run through me. He *shattered* that lock. What the hell else can he do?

The floorboards sag alarmingly beneath my feet, like the old wood is debating whether to give way, and the sensation jerks my mind back into focus. I'm trying not to think about the explosions. About the wolves or the collapsed ceiling or what else might've happened back there.

What could have gone wrong.

The shivers grow worse. *Ruby* might have been in that room when things went to hell.

Amar slows. Another tingle of static stings my arm where he holds it, this one fainter than the first. Almost cautious in a way, and the scarcely audible clink of metal that follows only reinforces that impression. Amar eases open a door, letting a sliver of light into the space around us.

The stench of sweat grows worse, as do all the other terrible smells. Amar inches forward, scanning the space beyond the doorway.

I peer past him. Unlike the area we left behind, the ground here is concrete. Fluorescent utility lights blaze overhead, though they're swaying from the aftereffects of the explosion minutes ago. And on the floor...

Cages. Maybe four-feet high, they're roofed in pocked, weathered concrete and walled with the same. Bars form their front, the metal so thick it looks like it's intended to stop rabid lions. The cages line both sides of the space, leaving only a walkway interrupted by rusty drains between them.

Warily, Amar steps away from the door, holding me at arm's length in the shadows for a moment before pulling me out after him. My eyes dart around only to stop when I see the far end of the room.

The ceiling is half gone. I knew it would be. But there are bodies too. A big man and two wolves on the ground. They don't move. There are cages beneath the destroyed ceiling as well, or there were. Chunks of metal stick out from concrete debris, like the roofs of the cages smashed downward under the collapsing weight from above.

I tremble. Ruby wouldn't have been there, though. She's *here,* not there.

A rustling comes from my left. My focus snaps back.

Whimpering sounds slip from the shadows of a cage. Desperate sounds. A hand follows, grasping the bars and dragging a man closer. He's middle-aged, maybe. Wearing a business suit or what's left of one. Mist tangles over his skin, weird and snakelike and sparking like wiring on the fritz. Eyes closed, he presses the side of his face to the bars, and his mouth gapes like he's gasping for air. Like he's drowning.

I jump when Amar's hand moves on my arm. I look back at him.

"Come on," he says.

I'm breathless, as if I've been running a marathon while standing still. "But—"

"We can't save them all."

I turn back to the man. His hand has slipped past the bars now. He's pawing at the air blindly, reaching for us.

"You don't know what these people did to end up here," Amar continues more firmly. "Alistair wasn't lying about that part. Not every one of them is innocent. Not by far."

My head shakes. I want to protest. To say it doesn't matter what they did: this isn't *justice*. Hell, this isn't even *sane*.

"People will be coming, Cait. I can't be the only one who spotted that side door."

Adrenaline tingles through my veins at the words, like I can already feel the guards chasing us. Nausea roils inside me, but I tear my focus from the man and scan the other cages.

"Ruby?" I call, trying to keep my voice down. "Ruby?"

A weird noise comes from ahead. Part mewling, part gasping, and all of it barely human. Trembling, I cross to the opposite side of the walkway.

Something moves in the shadows of one of the cages. Rustling, scratching, it doesn't come into the light.

I'm shaking so hard I can't breathe. "Ruby?"

An angry sound follows, sharp and short, and I flinch. Struggling to get a grip on myself, I force myself to inch closer. "Ru—"

The thing lunges forward, slamming into the bars. I jerk away.

And stare.

I want to scream. Cry. Maybe just wake up. Because this can't be Ruby. This can't be what they've done to her. She's snarling at us. Her green eyes are wild. Her filthy hands reach through the bars, clawing at me, at the air, at anything in reach. Her face is a mess of dirt and scratches, and the mist around her is speckled with shredded blue fragments. Everything from her clothes to her skin is covered in stains.

Brownish-red ones.

New fear shoots through my horror. "Is she hurt?" I start forward.

Amar catches my arm again. "She's not hurt."

His words are flat. Controlled. I glance up at him. He hasn't taken his eyes from Ruby, and confusion fills me at his stone-like expression. "But—"

"She's killed someone."

My mouth moves. Nothing comes out.

Reeling, I look back at Ruby. She's staring at me. She's still clawing toward us, but there's a desperation on her face now, like she's begging me to come over to her. Like she's in pain.

"She doesn't recognize you, Cait. She just knows what you are. That's why she wants you to come closer. Why that other guy did too. They can feel the magic in you. They want it."

My body shakes harder. I'm going to fall apart.

But not here.

Not yet.

The thought is stark and cold as ice, and it steadies me. I can crumble later. Cry later. Right now, I'm going to save my best friend.

No matter what.

"Can you fix this?" I force my voice to hold steady. "Like the—" I swallow hard. "Like I helped that other girl in the hospital. I don't know what I did, but can you—"

"Would she want us to?"

"*What?* Why would you—"

"This changes things." Amar's tone is measured. "She's killed somebody. She—"

"So does that mean you can't fix this? That *I* can't?"

His hand tightens on my arm, stopping me from going toward her. "It means she'll remember it. She'd remember everything else anyway, but now…" His mouth tightens, a dark and knowing look in his eyes that sends horrible shivers rippling through my core. "Now she'll remember whatever she did to that person as well."

I follow his gaze back to Ruby. Hungry sounds are escaping her. Frantic ones. Her mouth is moving in that same drowning, gasping motion as the other man, like she's trying to gulp down the air and who knows what else too.

"Would she want that?" Amar asks quietly. "The Touched tear people apart with their bare hands, Cait, and if she—"

I yank my arm from his grasp. This isn't happening. We're not having this discussion—the discussion of leaving her like this, deranged and inhuman. We're not considering *abandoning* her.

The shudders grow stronger. If I'd been just a *little* faster…

That thought isn't helping. We're here now. And Ruby…

My eyes go back to her. We're not leaving her. Not now. Not ever.

"Do it," I tell him. "Whatever you can do, just do it."

Amar hesitates, but then he nods. Carefully, he moves closer to Ruby.

A shriek leaves her, victorious and desperate all at the same time. Her hand flails out, snagging his arm, clenching down on it. I see him wince when her blood-stained nails dig at his skin.

He reaches out anyway, slipping his other hand past the bars and putting his palm to her cheek.

Joy floods her expression. My stomach churns at the

sight. Amar was right. She knows what he is. She expects him to feed her the mist.

Amar exhales like he's steadying himself. His gaze locks on Ruby, and her eyes go wide in response, alarm taking the place of her joy. She jerks back, trying to escape. Twisting his arm in her grasp quickly, he grabs her, trapping her by the bars.

She screams furiously. Shoving backward, she thrashes and kicks, her other hand ripping at Amar and her head twisting. She's attempting to bite him, I realize. Like a wild animal, she's trying to—

Her motions slow. The mist around her begins to fade, taking the snarled blue threads with it. Amar's grip tightens on her forearm, his whole body rigid with concentration while confusion and fear take the place of the alarm in her eyes, as if she's waking up to find herself still in a nightmare.

I recognize the look. The girl in the hospital had a similar expression.

"Ruby?" I try, coming closer.

She flinches like my voice hurts, and her head shakes as if to drive the sound away. Her face crumples, tears brimming in her eyes while her body sags against the bars.

Amar lets her go.

My eyes dart between them. "Is she… a-are you…" I don't know what to ask.

"I'm fine," Amar answers, sounding winded. "And she —" He shakes his head. "It's gone, anyway. Much of it as can be."

I look back at Ruby. She's lifting her hands in front of her. For a moment, she stares at them, blinking like she's slowly remembering they belong to her body before turning her eyes to her clothes.

She begins to shake. Her mouth opens, gaping soundlessly.

And then she starts to scream.

I'm moving instantly, falling to my knees by the cage. "Ruby! Ruby, you—"

She scrambles backward only to freeze when she sees me. Confusion twists her face. Horror too, like she can't understand how I can be here.

There's no reason she should.

"Get this door open," I demand of Amar. "Please, you have to—"

"What the hell are you *doing*?"

I turn at the furious shout. The man I thought was dead at the other end of the room is stumbling to his feet and glaring at me. His bald head is gashed, and the wound bleeds red trails down both sides of his face. He straightens like it's nothing, though. Like rage alone holds him upright.

And he's massive. Burly like a woodsman and wearing a rubber smock like a butcher. His hands flex as if practicing the grip they'll take on my throat, and he cracks his neck while he staggers toward me. "That's my *stock*! Keep your hands off the—"

Amar steps in front of me, and the man stops, his rage giving way to surprise. He runs his eyes over Amar, that same look coming onto his face that the people in the main room had. The one that says he can't believe Amar is here.

"You?" The man spits the word. "*You're* doing this?"

I look at Amar warily. Why do people keep reacting to him this way?

Amar doesn't say a word. A strange feeling spreads over my skin, like static is building in the air.

The man scoffs. "Try it, you freak. You think I'm scared

of you? I'm going to drag your ass to Lucretia and watch her tear you—"

A crashing sound cuts him short. I look back.

Shaking woodchips from its fur, a wolf steps from the debris of the door. Two more wolves pace through the shattered doorway behind it, their eyes sweeping the room and then locking on the man at the end of the walkway.

They growl. Every hair on my body stands on end from instinctive, primordial fear at the sound.

The man's lip curls with disgust. The static feeling in the air suddenly changes, like two competing sources are giving off the electricity now.

"Come on, you mangy runts," the man snarls. "I've already got two pelts to add to my collection. Come give me three m—"

Streaks of fur fly past me. A wolf slams into the man's chest, sending him staggering. The other two circle fast, their teeth going for the backs of his knees.

I turn away sharply. A scream rings from the walls, becoming a wet gurgle a second later.

Amar appears beside me. Without a word, he grabs the heavy lock holding the cage closed and tugs hard. The thing shatters like it's made of clay. In a quick motion, he tosses the debris aside and then yanks the door open.

Ruby stares at us both.

"We're here to help you." Amar extends a hand toward her. "There isn't much time."

"Please, Ruby," I beg when she doesn't move. "We have to get out of here."

I can see her trembling, but after a moment, she stretches her arm out warily.

Amar's fingers close around her hand, and he pulls her

forward. When she reaches the door, though, she hesitates. Her eyes slip toward the wolves.

"Don't." Amar moves, blocking her view. He looks at me, brief insistence flashing over his face like he's including me in the order.

I nod. The sounds I can hear from the opposite end of the room are terrible. I don't need to add visuals.

I feel sick enough as it is.

Amar draws something from his pocket and offers it to Ruby. "I need you to wear this."

My brow furrows at the strange pendant dangling from a necklace of black ribbon. It's delicate, a lacework of silver or maybe platinum. A pink stone glints unnaturally bright in the middle.

Distrust takes up residence on Ruby's face.

"It won't hurt you," Amar says. "I promise. It'll keep you safe for how we're going to get out of here."

Understanding clicks in my mind, but I don't know how to explain. What we're about to do is certain only to terrify her more. With her eyes almost—but not quite—twitching to me, Ruby takes the pendant warily.

"Now," Amar continues when she's put the necklace on. "I'm going to have to carry you, okay? You're going to be weak after all this, and we need to move fast."

Ruby gives a small nod.

He echoes the motion and then slips an arm below her legs. She wraps her arms around his neck, and then he hoists her from the ground.

"Close your eyes," he advises her, gentleness entering his tone. "It'll be easier."

She hesitates again and then does as he says.

Amar glances at me. "Doorway. Keep your hand on my arm."

I nod quickly and hurry after him when he strides toward the ruined doorway and the darkness there.

"Deep breath," Amar cautions.

I gasp in air.

We step forward, cross the line of shadow, and leave the place behind.

27

Even the cold white furniture of Bianca's penthouse feels welcoming after what we've just seen. Flames dance in the fireplace, casting glimmers of light from the glass coffee table. On the couch, the Dobermans have curled up on either side of Ruby like they can tell she needs the comfort, or maybe simply the sense of protection. It's belying every horror story I've heard about their breed.

But Ruby hasn't looked at me. Wrapped in a pale gray blanket, she's sat staring at the fire ever since we arrived. I want to say something to her.

I don't even know where to begin.

"Cait?"

I turn to find Amar standing beside the stiff armchair that's held me for the past fifteen minutes. He twitches his head toward the kitchen. "Can we talk to you?"

I nod. Pushing away from the chair, I cast another glance at Ruby.

She hasn't moved. She gives no sign she's noticed us at all.

Swallowing hard, I follow Amar through the doorway into the brightly lit kitchen. Bianca is there, leaning against the white counter with a solemn expression. The pink-stone pendant rests in a tangle of ribbon beside her.

"What?" I ask warily.

Amar glances at Bianca.

"Volgert," she says. "They're going to be furious. Amar can take care of himself, but you…"

I bite my lip. I'd worried it was something like this. Kyle and Volgert wouldn't let it go now that Ruby was back.

Now that half their "set" had been blown to pieces.

I wrap my arms around my middle. "Yeah. So what do we do?"

"First off, Bianca needs to teach you how to defend yourself," Amar says. "Soon. And as for Ruby…" His gaze slides to the living room like he's trying to choose the right words.

"There are going to be side effects," Bianca fills in bluntly.

A shiver ripples from the pit of my stomach. "What kind of side effects?"

Bianca shrugs. "Basically, your friend—"

She cuts off at the sound of the front door opening. Amar gives her a questioning glance and then heads toward the noise.

"What the hell?" I hear him demand when he reaches the living room.

I hurry out after him. The man with metal teeth is standing by the front door, his bald head shining in the firelight. On the couch, Ruby is staring at him. The two Dobermans are on their feet and growling at her side.

"Hey, hey." The man holds up his enormous hands. His

voice is a rumble, deep with bass. "No need to get excited."

Bianca strides from the kitchen behind me. "How the fuck did you get into my apartment?"

"Holes in your security. I patched them up."

"Leave," Amar orders. "Now."

The man shakes his head. "Not happening."

Glowing mist rushes up around Bianca's forearms, flaring brilliant pink and throwing off sparks. The air around us seems to come to life, crackling with enough static to electrocute someone. I hear Ruby make a panicked noise, but I can't take my eyes from the others.

"You heard him," Bianca growls.

The man doesn't lower his hands. "I'm not here for a fight."

"Then what do you want?" she demands.

"Oh, the same thing everyone else is going to want, now that you all showed your faces at that set tonight." He grins, turning his attention to me. "Cait."

AFTERWORD

**The Demon Guardians Series continues in
Demon Summoned!**

Love this story? Great! Would you please leave a review?
This helps me know what you enjoyed, and it also lets
others know what to look forward to! Please visit
BookBub, Goodreads, or any book-related site and tell
people about Demon Touched!

ACKNOWLEDGMENTS

The Demon Guardians series wouldn't be what it is today without the help of an incredible group of generous people to whom I owe tremendous thanks.

First and foremost, my mother and sister, who support the hell out of me at every turn. They've gotten me through bad times and dark times, and they never wavered in their love and care for even a moment. Thank you both. I'm so grateful you're in my life.

To my dear friend Robin Augsburg, thank you for your friendship and for putting up with my endless proofreading and grammar questions, as always. You're an absolute gift.

Thanks also go to my friend and fellow author, Sara Whitney, for beta-reading, for talking out ideas with me, and for her suggestions for this series. Your insight is deeply appreciated. Thank you.

To Veronica, the sensitivity reader at Salt and Sage, thank you for your invaluable input and recommendations. I greatly appreciate your time in reading and your thoughts on this story. Thank you as well to Erin Olds, owner of Salt and Sage, for all your efforts in coordinating the sensitivity read. I'm grateful for you both.

Thanks as well to the many talented authors of my RWA chapter for their input and to my reader group on Facebook for their support. You all are amazing.

ABOUT SKYE MALONE

Skye Malone writes action-packed fantasy and paranormal romance. A fan of magical books since childhood, they adore stories that pit ordinary characters against extraordinary odds and reveal the strength within. Abandoned buildings are their passion, along with old castles and deep, dark parts of the forest where anything is possible. A graduate of the University of Illinois with a degree in English literature, Skye lives in the Midwest with a retired racing greyhound and a three-legged mutt.

Join Skye Malone's mailing list to receive a free story and to hear about all Skye's new releases, sales, and giveaways. Visit skyemalone.com/mailinglist today!

amazon.com/author/skyemalone

bookbub.com/authors/skye-malone

goodreads.com/skyemalone

facebook.com/authorskyemalone

twitter.com/Skye_Malone

instagram.com/authorskyemalone